# Miss Lionheart & the Laboratory of Death

First edition 2016

Phantom Feather Press © 2014
29 Laura Ave, Brooklyn, Wellington 6021,
New Zealand
phantomfeatherpress@gmail.com

## Dedication

To all the people without whom this book would not have been possible – my family, my fellow writers, and Imojen.
Thank you.

## WWWOE Rules

No 1: Don't be noticed –
but if you are, create a lasting impression

No 2: When you're the boss, you can write your own rules

No 3: There are no rules – as long as you don't get caught

# CONTENTS

## Part I- Once Bitten


1 The Offer 9
2 Mr Big's Hideout 15
3 The Menagerie 23
4 Dr Deathless 28
5 Uncertainty – Also Known as the Uncertainty Clause 33
6 In or Out? 40
7 Snakes, Rats and Spider Venom 47
8 Don't Panic 52
9 Panic 62
10 Hope 70
11 Threatened 74
12 Twice Shy 83


## Part II - Twice Poisoned


13 Laying Low 96
14 The Experiment 106
15 Quetzee 113

16 The Appetizer 123

17 Help 129

18 Paul the Poisoner 138

19 Christmas in an Evil Criminal Mastermind's Bunker 150

20 An Unexpected and Unwelcome Christmas Present 155

## Part III - Thrice Shy

21 Monster Death Ring 166

22 Betrayed 172

23 Down a Rabbit Hole 184

24 When your Whole World is Black 189

25 The Hatching 194

26 The Issue 199

27 Greed 204

28 Pride 211

29 Death 221

30 Fall 229

# PART I - ONCE BITTEN

•1•

# THE OFFER

LILLY GLANCED BEHIND. A black car with heavily-tinted windows turned the corner – the thud of pop music on its stereo turned up too loud to ignore.

The vehicle screeched to a stop and began following her with a slow deliberateness. The thud thud thud of her heart began to war with the syncopated drum-track.

A terrible wailing of synthesised voice blasted from the car's stereo, as the vehicle drove up onto the curb in front of her.

Bullies from school?

Lilly gnawed the inside of her cheek with a familiar anticipation. Someone was about to get seriously hurt – and it was going to be very hard to explain later.

Expecting the usual taunts, *Miss lah de dah Professor thinks she's sooo special, swanning around at the looni-versity*, and, *look, it's the mutant freak*, Lilly was surprised when two thugs in black leathers jumped out without saying a word. With their shaved heads, meaty palms and identical bulldog expressions, the pair were almost indistinguishable – except the first glowed an unhealthy radioactive greyish brown, and the second was so pale his blue veins stood out under his skin. Odd.

Concentrate. What else?

They were young, in their twenties at most, and plastered with crime syndicate patches, including the internationally feared WorldWideWebOfEvil.com

Definitely not from school then.

Lilly breathed deeply. The first thing she learnt in spy school was, *don't show them you're afraid*. And the best way to do that was not to be afraid.

She took half a step toward the two boys, kicked off a rather expensive pair of heels, and ran. Not because she was frightened – of course not – if these guys were trying to kill her, she'd already be dead. It was the soul-destroying thought of having to listen to the whine of the singer from the car's stereo for a moment longer. That, and she abhorred their leathers. Not just for the lack of dress sense, but because animals looked so much better in their own skins.

The two thugs walked after her unhurriedly. Good, there was no way they could catch her at that speed. They started jogging, still far too slow.

She had her escape plan mapped out (through a nearby garden and over the fence) when the car revved. It reversed past, with a screech of tyres, and once again blocked the path in front of her.

She spun around. Seriously? How many people were after her? Three? Four? She tried to race past the two thugs, onto the empty road.

They pushed her back with surprising strength, their hands burning cold.

Lilly's stomach lurched. Those hands were too cold to be alive. Her brain rebelled. Undead? Impossible. But they *had* to be.

She should be doing something clever to escape, but couldn't think of any good options. She couldn't even pretend she wasn't frightened any more. Instead of figuring out a plan, her brain was stuck on the undead question.

From inside the car someone growled, "Mr Big has a job for you."

"Mr Big?" Lilly echoed, trying to give herself more time to think. As head of Global Killing Systems (GKS) Laboratories he was one of the least important crime lords – and the most dangerously unpredictable.

One of the half-frozen thugs grabbed her arm in a chillingly vice-like grip and yanked her toward the car.

Folded into the back seat was a cauliflower-eared brute, squashed into a pinstripe suit, his tiny pin-sized head incongruous with the rest of his bulk. "It will only take a moment."

"I'm a bit busy," she replied, trying to extricate herself from the thug's iron grip by breaking his fingers. A couple of short sharp snaps and … nothing. He didn't even seem to notice.

The oaf in the pinstripes smiled. "Miss Lionheart. Miss Lilliana Lionheart. Please don't damage my two colleagues here. They're rather expensive. Besides, I don't think you understand. Mr Big wants you to be an integral part of the GKS laboratory's biological division."

"Yeah, and what Mr Big wants, Mr Big gets," sneered the blue-veined boy.

"Hush Veins," the oaf in pinstripes said. "Talking's my job, remember?"

Heart hammering, Lilly shook her head. "You've made a mistake. I'm just a school kid. Whoever it is you're after, it's not me."

Pinhead[1] pulled out a plastic folder with **MISS LILLIANA LIONHEART** on the cover. He smiled as he flourished her grades, a passport, and a picture of Embraldo, the pet lizard-gecko hybrid she'd created when she was younger.

Much younger, she thought, biting at the inside of her

1 Lilly decided Pinhead was as good a name as any for the muscled oaf in the pinstripes with a head at least two sizes too small.

cheeks to stop herself from saying something that would make the man angry. *Angrier.* He seemed pretty angry already.

"Mr Big has organised a meeting, so come along nice, or say goodbye to that pretty face of yours."

Lilly tried to tell herself it was an empty threat. She tried to barge past the two thugs – and failed as they blocked her escape, again.

She hit out and screamed, for all the good it did. Nobody could possibly hear her over the high-pitched music.

This time, when Pinhead spoke, he wasn't laughing or smiling, or even asking nicely. "Hurry up and get in," he growled. "We've wasted enough time here."

"What?" Lilly said, pretending not to hear him. "Um, I don't suppose I could grab my shoes?"

"These?" Basher said, picking a shoe up with his thumb and forefinger, and tearing it apart.

Crying wasn't an option, so slowly, carefully, she slipped her hand into her pocket and began to text home. She needed to keep talking to distract these idiots. "I have to go, I'm late for Biochemistry, it's a fascinating lecture on the interactions of messenger RNA."

"Get in now!" he thundered. "Or you won't like the consequences."

"I tell you what I don't like," Lilly said, giving up on deaf and trying for a bravado she didn't quite feel. "People telling me what to do."

She'd almost finished typing a message with the car's licence number, *M1N1NSRUS*, into her phone. Knowing she wasn't the fastest stealth texter, she kept talking. "Besides, I hate your choice of musak. Isn't there something else you could harass me with? Mr Goodie's Band and his Bad Time Hits? Top Dog and the Strangled Cats?"

Veins smacked his near transparent fist against his meaty palm.

His grey-brown double snapped, "Come on, let's just bash her over the head and shove her in the boot."

"Nah, Basher," growled Pinhead. "You know what Mr Big said. Shut up, while I try to do this proper-like."

"How about we do the other usual?" Veins growled. He clenched his fists so hard his veins popped into stark blue-green relief. "This is boring."

Having completed typing what Lilly hoped was, *Help! M1N1NSRUS Mr Big*, she tried to hit the send button.

Basher ripped her hand from her pocket. "Keep those hands where I can see them," he growled.

Lilly tried not to groan. She could hit send later – hopefully. Right now, the cold barrel of a gun pushed against her head was taking all her attention.

"Get into the car or I'll blow your brains out," Pinhead snapped.

Smiling meekly, (despite a horde of brutal, if imaginary, butterflies, tearing her stomach apart) Lilly raised her hands and stepped into the car. After all, what else could she do? The offer had been made with such eloquence and conviction, she couldn't exactly refuse.

# Join The World Wide Web of Evil Today!

With a chance to become an evil mastermind, this is a career opportunity you should never turn down. Start working in an evil crime syndicate today.
The World Wide Web of Evil offers a steady job for life, and the chance to work in safely-fortified bunkers in all parts of the globe.

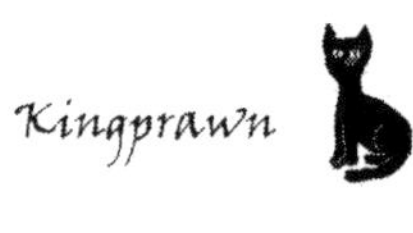

Check out all the famous villains that started their career with us. And just think, you can too!

Professor Horrible's
Evil Equine
Enterprises

Yes, that's right, when the rest of the world turns its head away, The World Wide Web of Evil is ready to pick up the pieces. We're there to create the employment opportunities you are seeking. So join us now! We're seeking scientists, minions, explosive experts, cooks, muscle and more ... Opportunities are available for almost every expertise and level of experience.

Mr Xu

Dr Doomed

Big Brother

Join up right now at-
misslillylionheart.wordpress.com/join-us-at-the-wwwoe

flyer courtesy of WWWOE propaganda division

Call the WWWOE today at ██████

•2•

# MR BIG'S HIDEOUT

LILLY WAS BLINDFOLDED AND driven a short way, then led through a convoluted underground maze at gunpoint. It felt surreal, as if she'd been captured by an amateur drama production. Or as if she wasn't trudging through an underground bunker at all, but listening from far away. Still, she did manage to send her text message (M1N1NSRUS Mr Big) and stay focused, the way her endless spy training had reinforced. Carefully counting every step, Lilly took note of the *shhh* of automatic doors, the *whoosh* of walls sliding open, and the grating sound of rotating fireplaces. She heard strange cracks and pops, and a loud hum like electricity, which stopped abruptly as they raced over a cold metal floor that clanged with the guards' footsteps. Weird.

Not long after, the blindfold was lifted and she found herself face to face with a puffed up man in an expensive suit. He was surrounded by guards, and holding tightly to the collar of a giant Rottweiler.

Presumably this was Mr Big, the man who'd ordered her capture. She wanted to say the exact right thing to get herself out of this mess. But now she'd seen him, that was impossible. Either she was useful, or she was dead. Best to just relax and not think at all. *Be calm, be ready, don't over-think it and smile*, just like she'd been taught. Only this was life or death.

She was shoved forward. "Mr Big, this is Miss Lionheart."

Jovial as Father Christmas, Mr Big grinned and stretched out the hand that wasn't holding back the overgrown Rottweiler. "Hello, Miss Lionheart, pleased to meet you. I'm Mr Big." He shook her hand until her whole arm hurt.

When she was young, she'd imagined all super-villains to be much the same – a penchant for dangerous animals and an ego big enough to collapse a white star. It was somewhat of a disappointment to discover her younger self had been right.

He finally released her aching arm. "And *this*, is Annie. She's wonderful, isn't she?"

Annie growled. Scarred, distempered and very toothy – she was the type of Rottweiler that would eat your babies for breakfast, and come back for a second helping of postman.

"Delightful," Lilly said, trying to pet Annie while sizing up the guards. Annie snapped at her hand and growled more fiercely than ever.

"Good girl." Mr Big patted Annie genially, oblivious of the froth dripping from her agitated jaw. "Miss Lionheart, I see you have a way with animals. Fantastic. And what a wonderful co-incidence: here you are, when I just happen to need a head genetic engineer. We desperately need someone to lead the team designing the mutant animal section of my Spring Catalogue of Evil, and you'll be the perfect fit."

"But … " Lilly tried to object. Fists clenched with a mix of terror and barely restrained anger.

"Of course it's a great honour. I do so hope you'll say yes." He smiled in a way that was probably meant to be reassuring. "I'm sure that you understand the lack of ceremony. I had to fill this auspicious position at the last possible moment because, unfortunately, my previous head of department died of mange."

A guard even larger than Pinhead frowned. "I thought you shot him, sir."

Mr Big scowled and tugged Annie's collar before releasing it. Quick as lightning, Annie leapt up and took the guard by the jugular. Blood gushed, bones cracked, and his body hit the floor with the force of a small atom bomb.

"Is he dead?" Lilly asked, shock overwhelming any sense of decorum.

"Not yet." Mr Big looked at his watch. "In three, two … one … now."

Lilly almost gagged as Annie crunched into the man's cervical vertebrae – or neck bones if you prefer the non-scientific term. Lilly always preferred science when considering prodigious quantities of gore.

Mr Big looked up from the carnage.

"You did say yes, didn't you, young lady?"

Lilly didn't move.

He waved his hand in annoyance. "I'll take that as a yes. Pat, Miss Lionheart needs to get to her lab." He raised his voice over the sound of crunching, slobbering dog. "And little Miss, I want my dreadbeast last week, understand?"

Pinhead nodded, and Lilly barely had time to register the man she thought of as Pinhead was called Pat, before he, Veins and Basher pushed her out of the room, down a corridor and through a set of double doors labelled, *Super Evil Genius' Laboratory.* Inside, amongst *very* expensive equipment, a boy rocked back and forth on a lab stool. All of about twelve, he had curly hair, glasses, and a serious expression.

He looked up at her. "Hi, I am Squidge."

Lilly could have sworn his eyes were focused at a point just over her shoulder. Maybe Pinhead was freaking him out.

She smiled and stuck out her hand. "Hi, I'm Lilly."

He ignored it. "No, you are Miss Lionheart. Mr Big said so."

"Um," Lilly shrugged. "I guess I am. Aren't you a little young to be – ?"

He flinched away. "I am fourteen tomorrow. Besides, Prof could not have run this lab without me. It is a shame he died. The man was absolutely brilliant, you know. He always said so. Besides, his plans are the most fantastic things you will ever see." He shoved a large sketchbook up to Lilly's nose. "This is the dreadbeast we are going to make! It is brilliant! Absolutely brilliant!"

"Lovely." Lilly cringed, the sketches looked more like notes from a graphic novel than a scientific document – plenty of human corpses in full gory detail, but no understanding about the clash between arachnid and reptilian physiology. And most damningly, no sense of balance. The creature, with its enormous abdomen and overlarge jaws, would struggle to walk. If indeed, it could live at all.

Lilly's phone rang – and she jumped. Why hadn't she turned it to vibrate?

"You'd better answer that," Pinhead said. Was he smirking?

She glanced at her phone: *GKS security division: Regards your previous message, may we be of assistance?*

Lilly did her best to ignore the roars of laughter coming from Pinhead. Served her right for not sending it earlier. It was time to get her head in the game. "And how do you know your Prof was – er brilliant?" she asked, flicking through pages of increasingly bizarre creatures before stopping at a drawing of a fire-breathing dragon – handwritten notes scrawled over every spare inch.

Squidge blinked owlishly behind his glasses. "Because that is what he told me."

"Well, I'm even more brilliant. I'm the most brilliant biologist that's ever been in this base. Far cleverer than your old Prof – just ask—" she looked around "—any of my teachers," she finished lamely. "Anyway, your Prof? What was he a professor in? Biology, Physics, Chemistry?"

The boy smiled. "Philosophy."

"Philosophy? Surely you mean philosophy of science?" she asked.

Squidge looked at her as if she was stupider than a common household brick. "Philosophical philosophy," he said, and glanced away.

"Great," Lilly replied, with a grin more false than a fat-free label on a candy bar. She flicked back to the page labelled, *Dreadbeast.* It didn't fill her with any hope. However scary this dreadbeast might be – in its giant mutant spider way, with hundreds of eyes, oversized claws, and forked tongue – the probability, the near certainty of not creating it scared her far more. The fear of informing her new Super-villain boss that she couldn't make his dreadbeast, weighed like a stone in water, like a church bell at an intimate concrete funeral. Or, more precisely, like the thought of becoming part of an all-you-can-eat Rottweiler buffet.

Anxious to avoid such a fate, she looked carefully at Prof's scrawled notes. And considering failure was not an option, the more she looked, the more possibilities she saw. She just had to think outside the box – or more precisely figure out how to get outside the box she was in. Yes, while the creature she was looking at had to be ninety-nine tenths of impossible, maybe she could make a different type of lethal animal while she was figuring out how to escape.

Squidge interrupted her thoughts. "Miss Lionheart, the dreadbeast is going to be our biggest and best creature yet. The greatest mutant evil companion a supervillain has ever had."

"Our?" she asked, ignoring the whole supervillain mutant companion bit. "Our? And what do you do?"

"Most everything," Squidge replied.

"But you're—"

"I have a Doctorate in Biochemical Genetics." He waved at his Oxford, *Doctor of Philosophy* certificate hanging on the wall.

"Great." Lilly smiled through gritted teeth, trying to figure out if she was angry because Squidge was a little bit stupid, or because he had a doctorate and she didn't. "Is there anything else I should know? For a start, when do I get to go home? Mr Big seems to have missed that little detail."

"Home?" Squidge said. "Nobody goes home."

Behind them, Pinhead laughed. She turned around and stepped right up to his chin. "What's so funny?"

"Nothing, Miss Lionheart. It's just – the boss had very strict instructions. He said, 'the only way that Miss Lionheart is getting out of this bunker is in a body bag.'"

Veins, Basher and Pinhead were all laughing now.

"Hmmm," Lilly said, seeing an opportunity to escape. She knew some drugs that could fake death quite nicely.

"Ha ha. Good joke. The boss has not used a body bag since I arrived." Squidge said, oblivious that her newly hatched dream of escape was being crushed. "How silly to throw dead people out on the street when we have all these animals that need feeding."

Lilly tried not to wince. She couldn't help but think this was all her fault. If only she hadn't chosen to study Biology, believing it would be a much safer career path than becoming a spy. (Much to the disgust of her school counsellor and parents, who'd insisted she complete *Spy Survival 320*).

Squidge picked up the picture of the dreadbeast again. "See how beautiful it is. And dangerous. Mr Big wants it to be his new company emblem."

She blinked. "I'll draw a nice picture for him."

"Don't be silly. Mr Big likes his emblems to be real. He is going to christen the New Year by letting it loose in Professor

Horrible's lair."

"What?" Lilly grabbed the picture and tried to soak in its stupendous lack of practicality. "He wants us to make this thing before the New Year? This is a joke, right? I mean Christmas is only weeks away."

Nobody smiled.

She coughed, trying to clear her rapidly constricting throat. Somehow, she had to escape an impregnable fortress, make an impossible creature – or die.

This could not be happening.

As a child she'd learnt early that screaming could often get you what you want. It hadn't worked earlier that day, but there was no harm in trying again. Lilly opened her mouth to make a scene – when something screeched, but not her. It seemed to be coming from a room further down the corridor. More animals joined in the cacophony.

In sheer frustration, Lilly decided to scream anyway.

Nobody noticed. Squidge was already running down the corridor, and the guards were pushing past her to do the same.

Sometimes there are no good options. She sighed, and ran toward the terrible sound.

§

To: Flynn@MrBig.net.www.e
From: Untraceable
Subject: Urgent
Time: Dec 3, 16:27

Send the note: "Are you Schrodinger's Cat?"

# Join the World Wide Web of Spies Today!

Have you always longed for excitement and almost certain death? The WWWOS is a career path that will almost certainly take you to the pearly gates of heaven – but what a way to go! Cool gadgets, fast cars, champagne, expensive suits, and even more expensive hotels. The WWWOS will give you the chance to live like a rock star, all while saving your country from the plague of the WWWOE. Don't miss this twice-a-year opportunity to become one of our top undercover agents. You know you're worth it – and besides, after our grueling fitness program you'll look so great, everybody will be watching your every step. Join us now!

misslillylionheart.wordpress.com/join-us-at-the-wwwos

**Terms and conditions:**
We have the best retirement plans in the world – check them out, and then decide which castle or resort you want to end your days in. We have four of our five available castles vacant right now! In addition, our government funded "death in the line of duty" pension will likely feed your family for months – or at least until the next wave of inflation. Really, why are you still reading? Don't you trust us?

**Microdot**
**Terms and Conditions**

**Please note: champagne, expensive suits, hotels, and all other sundries may or may not apply (and usually don't). But if you have managed to read this advisory, we think you are more suited to an administrative role. The hours are better, the pay is better, and there's a lot less dying involved. So why not join as at www.s today and apply for a boring technician or administration role?**

# •3•

# THE MENAGERIE

**DOZENS OF ENORMOUS EYES,** decorated with silvery electronics and flashing diodes, floated down the corridor. Each was balanced on top of some kind of helium bag, with a tiny fan on the rear, swishing back and forth like a malformed tail. They brushed past Lilly as if she wasn't there, and flocked toward a cacophony of distressed animals behind a double door with *Mena* stencilled on one side, and *gerie* on the other.

As Squidge opened the doors, Lilly gagged and pressed her hand across her mouth. It was as if the gates of hell had opened to disgorge the reek of death, chemicals, faeces, and wet animal fur in an overwhelming miasma. She stood horrified – and yet the scene before her was also a revelation in amazing.

Blinking, Lilly tried to take it all in.

Hundreds of creatures, packed into cages lining the walls, were kicking up a fuss. An unhappy lion, his fur falling off in hanks, roared fit to wake the dead – and kill them again. Elephants, monkeys, hyenas, monitor lizards, snakes and more, all terrified by two idiots in overlarge yellow parkas and gloves, squirting a hose haphazardly about.

Lilly strained to see through the spray. She ran forward to get a closer look – were those rare hybrids? Yes – ligers, cabbits,

Simian rat monkeys and genetically-engineered giant mice carrying human arms and legs and other appendages on their backs.

Squidge ran beside her through the chaos, yelling as the two workers continued to jet streams of frothy water into the animals' cages. A feathered creature screamed, clattering an oversized claw against the bars of its cage. Strangely familiar, it was as much bird as dinosaur. Velociraptor?

There were more dinosaurs up ahead. And giant insects scraping their legs and rasping their mandibles in fear.

Lilly couldn't follow what Squidge was saying over the racket. But she did hear one thing. "*...mites....*"

The Prof's mange! Of course. The fools in yellow coats were squirting insecticide into a room full of insects and other sensitive creatures. "Stop!" she screamed, trying to be heard over the racket. "Stop right now. That spray's lethal. You're killing them!"

"What?" Squidge yelled back.

The two minions mustn't have heard either. Oblivious as they moved closer and closer to the giant insects, wreaking havoc.

Miniature pink and blue ponies were picked up by the spray and sent tumbling into the back of their cage.

Frantic, Lilly grabbed a small empty cage, and threw it.

The cage bounced and skittered into the legs of the two sprayers. They turned off their hoses and swung around, stomping toward her like aliens from a horror movie – their heavy coats belling, and their faces in WWWOE black-tinted face masks designed to hide every recognisable feature.

Lilly took a small step back.

Run? Never. Her feet were getting rather sore, and besides, animals' lives were at stake.

Heart thumping, she stood her ground until the pair stood toe to toe with her – and ripped off their masks.

The illusion of aliens was shattered. The faces glaring back at her were young. One was a girl, probably not much older than her. Seventeen? Eighteen? It was hard to tell – her pale face was cast in jaundice-yellow from her coat. The other, a boy, pushed back his hood to reveal a healthier looking skin tone. "What the hell!" he yelled, a mop of tousled blond hair flopping over his eyes.

Lilly wasn't about to back down. Lives depended on it. She stepped right up to him, until she was an inch away from his face. "What the hell, yourself? What exactly do you think you're doing?"

"Following orders," the boy shrugged. "Doctor Deathless said we needed to spray for mange."

Lilly took a deep breath. "I'm running this lab now. Not this Doctor whoever. And I'm running it properly. So who are you to tell me what to do?"

The boy looked at Squidge.

Squidge nodded.

"Oh." The boy smiled ruefully from under his mop of unruly hair and extended his arm. "Hi, I'm Brian, and this is Missy. She's shy."

"Her name is Melissa," Squidge said absently.

"And your name is Esquire Grey, but nobody calls you that." Brian clapped Squidge on the back. "Not even you."

Squidge glared.

"I— I— don't mind," Missy stammered, looking at the floor. A long twist of midnight black hair escaped her hood.

"Oh, hi Melissa … Missy … I'm Lilliana Lionheart, but everyone calls me Lilly." She held out her hand uncertainly.

"I do not," Squidge said. "I call her Miss Lionheart. She is taking over from Prof."

Missy and Brian looked at Lilly's outstretched hand as if it might bite. She casually dropped it back to the safety of her pockets and pretended not to be annoyed – after all they were just two kids following orders. "So, Missy and Brian. Are you with my lab permanently?"

They nodded.

"Hmmm. I don't suppose either of you know anything about animals?"

"I *like* animals," Missy piped up, her eyes flicking nervously toward the door. "That's why I applied for the job when I saw it advertised at the pet shop." She pulled a crumpled piece of paper from her pocket.[2]

**Love Animals?**

Why not apply to work in our state-of-the-art pet shop. Every animal you could ever wish for, big, small, furry, cuddly and with claws.

Email your CV today to petshop@www.e and we'll be in touch with more information about this amazing opportunity.

Lilly shook her head. "You haven't done any genetic research?"

Missy and Brian looked at each other.

"DNA sequencing? Any lab technician work at all?"

Brian managed to rake his hair out of his eyes. "Er, no, we just started today." The hair flopped back into place.

"So this is everyone? There aren't a few more technicians tucked out the back?" Lilly asked hopefully.

The two shrugged, and shook their heads.

"So let me see, I have two unqualified assistants who *like* animals, and a genius who doesn't like people. Great." Lilly

2 *VF*, your virtual friend says, *please avoid www.e or www.s sites, and direct all correspondence through misslillylioheart.wordpress.com*

scowled. “I’ll make things easier and go and kill myself now, shall I?”

Squidge did his best to laugh. “Ha, ha, Miss Lionheart. You are being funny again.”

“No.” Lilly glared at him, and then sighed as she saw the downcast faces of her assistants. “Oh never mind.” Just because she was having a bad day was no reason to make their lives even more miserable. She wondered briefly if the big cats she’d seen earlier would make a useful diversion for an escape attempt. No. Not nearly scary enough. A giant gorilla? No. It’d have to be over twenty metres high, and that would be too tall to even fit even this enormous building.

Somehow, Lilly forced a smile. “Let’s get rid of the worst of this mess, shall we? Then we can treat the animals properly tomorrow.”

As Brian and Missy nodded contritely, the door crashed open. In burst a wild-haired man in walk shorts, sandals, long socks, and a wide brown tie.

“D— D— D— Doctor Deathless,” Squidge said, and hid behind Missy.

§

To: Security@MrBig.net.www.e
From: MrBig@MrBig.net.www.e
Subject: Lion
Time: Dec 3, 16:34

Keep a close eye on our newest employee. In terror gate any won outside her lab that tries to contract her. Be vigilante, she has a known association with WWWOS.

Security

•4•

# DR DEATHLESS

LILLY LOOKED **DR DEATHLESS** up and down. He couldn't be half as crazy as he looked, could he? The fact that his fashion sense was over thirty years out of date, was hardly a recommendation.

"Squidge, you're going to be for the chop now, boy," he spat through his straggly beard. "You and your stupid lab. The only reason you're here is because the boss is crazy enough to think kids barely out of diapers can pull off the scientific breakthrough of a lifetime. But it won't be long now." He drew his finger across his beard. "Ggkh."

Lilly, regretting the loss of her shoes, pulled herself up to her full five foot three inches. "And who are *you* to order these two to spray insecticide through *my* lab?"

He held out his hand. "Dr John Deathless. Chief research coordinator of this facility."

"Ignore him," Squidge said. "He *was* the guy in charge, but he has not invented anything for decades. He is a washed up has-been, trading on old glory and re-animating the occasional zombie. Problem is, the boss figured this loser out a long time ago. That is why we are here."

Dr Deathless grabbed Squidge by the collar, and shook. "Moronic child, stop repeating that nonsense. You don't know anything. See, if I die, I've wired this place to blow. You clever enough to understand that, genius boy?"

"What?!" Lilly asked. "A bomb?!"

Nobody took any notice of Dr Deathless' threat. Or maybe nobody heard over Squidge screaming, "He invaded my personal space! He is touching me!" Squidge batted at the liver-spotted hands wrapped tightly around his neck.

Brian took half a step toward Squidge, as if to rescue him – then stopped.

Missy was not so easily cowed. "Get away from him!" she yelled, trying to push Deathless away.

"Yeah," Lilly said. "He's half your size."

Turning to the girls, Dr Deathless yelled back. "You kid geniuses come in thinking you're the best, but you all go just as fast as you arrive."

"I hope so," Lilly said, walking toward him.

Dr Deathless threw back his head and laughed.

"I don't think anything about this is very funny," Lilly said, raising her arm for a feint, as if intending to hit him, and readied herself to trip the bully. "Let go of Squidge, and tell me about this bomb."

The lab doors crashed open again, and a dragon-tattooed woman burst into the room. Twice as large and muscled as Pat Pinhead, she had the gait and determination of a Sumo wrestler. "What's going on here, then?" she asked.

"Hi, Deva," Dr Deathless said. "Nice of you to come join us."

About time, Lilly thought, as Deva kept on walking, the enormous dragon tattoos on her arms rippling with every step. It was a relief to see there was some kind of check being kept on this lunatic.

Dr Deathless waited until she was an arm's length away, and shoved Squidge.

Released, Squidge fell forward, covering his throat protectively with his hands.

"Squidge, you okay?" Lilly whispered.

Raising his arms above his head in mock surrender, Dr Deathless turned on his heel, muttering ominous warnings into his beard about bombs and revenge.

Deva stepped aside as he passed, then trailed warily in the man's wake, as if he was poisonous, or as if his crazy was catching.

It made Lilly so angry. How could that maniac be allowed anywhere near the menagerie, when he threatened to kill everything he came near?

Missy ditched her yellow coat. No longer jaundice yellow, her pale skin set off her sad, dark eyes. "It's alright. It's alright," she murmured soothingly to Squidge. "He's gone now."

"Personal space!" Squidge yelled at her. Arms curled around his stomach, he rocked back and forth. "I do not like people too close."

"Never mind that," Lilly snapped. "Half our critters are about to die."

Squidge only wrapped his arms about himself tighter.

"What?" Brian asked. "You're worried about the animals when Dr Deathless has strangled Squidge and threatened to blow up the menagerie?"

"Of course. Keeping animals is an important responsibility."

"Um," Missy said. "Brian, you do know Deathless hasn't just wired the menagerie – he's wired the whole bunker. At least that's what I heard."

"Evacuating excrement!" Lilly swore. It was another good reason to get out of here. Still, she had a duty to the animals that were under her care – however temporarily. "Look, I know Dr Deathless is scary, but we can't let ourselves be distracted. Otherwise some of our critters are going to get very sick, maybe even die."

Squidge shrugged. "If you are worried about the insecticide, we can turn on the sprinkler system and wash it away."

Missy and Brian nodded.

"No." Lilly folded her arms. "Even low levels of insecticide could kill every arthropod[3] in this place."

Squidge disentangled himself from his huddle on the floor and shrugged. "You are exaggerating. Maybe half of them. And even if we did lose every single one, they do not cost much to replace."

"What!?" Lilly demanded.

"Yeah … um … what's an arthropod?" Brian flicked back his hair. "Is that like an insect?"

"Mostly," Lilly said with a sigh. "Just try to remember there are all sorts of critters in the world that aren't mammals, and you'll do okay."

Spitting angry, she turned to Squidge. "Did you say living creatures don't cost much to replace?" she demanded. Ignorance was one thing, but his callous disregard was another. "Bad enough you've told the boss we can make this impossible dreadbeast, but—"

Squidge stepped back. "The dreadbeast is not impossible."

"Don't be crazy! Of course it is—" Lilly was about to say exactly why it was impossible, when she heard a soft whirring noise. One of the big silver eyes she'd seen earlier was hovering only an arm's length away. A tiny fan swishing its malformed tail back and forth.

Lilly took a step back.

The contraption hummed as it kept its distance, the eye staring at her eerily. It was horrible. She remembered laughing at her parents' outrage when she had been caught bugging her little brother's room. Maybe they'd been right, and keeping a close on eye on the little brat was a violation of privacy and out of line.

Nah.

---

3 An arthropod is an invertibrate with an exoskeleton (external skeleton). This group includes insects, spiders and mites. *LL*

Besides, this wasn't the time for introspection. She needed to think fast. And keep her trap closed about what she thought of Mr Big's project. The time for her to voice her reservations about his dreadbeast would be well after she'd escaped. Until then, her best chance of survival was to convince Squidge that a small success was better than a big failure. "Er, um, what I meant, Squidge, is, well, maybe we could start with something easier, just to kick things off."

Squidge knuckled his forehead, then grinned. "Of course! A test subject to get you used to our equipment. What about a simple bear-cat hybrid?"

"What? Simple?" Lilly gasped. "Um." Surely they could make something easier than that. "How about a snake-hybrid instead? I've always wanted to try one."

"Brilliant!" Squidge jumped up and down, flapping his arms in excitement. "Making the dreadbeast will be much easier after you are acclimated to the lab. I have—"

"Great plan." Lilly smiled. "But we're a little off track. Right now, we have animals to save. Let's get to work!"

Nobody moved.

A silver camera eye whirred as it manoeuvred around Lilly.

"We need to move some of these insect cages, and maybe the amphibians and reptiles. Squidge, I don't suppose you know if dinosaurs are susceptible to insecticide?"

Squidge folded his arms and didn't move. "Who cares? Dinosaurs are too erratic to be of any use anyway."

"What did you say?" Lilly asked in her best approximation of menacing.

"I said, who cares?" Squidge repeated calmly.

Before Lilly could react with the appropriate outrage, the door burst open again.

What now? Lilly thought as Pat Pinhead swaggered in, shadowed by the two zombies, Veins and Basher.

# •5•

# UNCERTAINTY-
# ALSO KNOWN AS THE UNCERTAINTY CLAUSE

On either side of the enormous pinstriped thug, Veins and Basher crashed their palms into their fists.

Lilly shivered. On the positive side, Dr Deathless' zombies weren't ripping up the furniture and demanding *brains*. On the negative side, she wondered if the brain-eating kind of zombie might be easier to deal with. And they'd somewhat mess up Pinhead's annoying suit – even if they couldn't manage to mess up the annoying bully himself.

"You listening, girl?" Pinhead demanded.

Lilly forced herself to concentrate through the whine of the all too obvious surveillance as it floated by.

"I don't like you," he said, pointing a meaty finger at her chest. "You're nothing but paperwork. So the sooner you're dead, the happier I'll be. But in the meantime, the rest of you." He looked about at Missy, Brian and Squidge. "Miss Lionheart is your new boss, so step to it, and get to work! Now!

*Her* staff jumped to it like they'd been electrocuted. It didn't exactly make Lilly feel any better. Obviously she wasn't really the boss. She was just a puppet, and this evil, brainless thug had more authority than she did.

She had an urge to attack him, entertaining the thought

of hitting him for all she was worth. She might not win, but she should be able to use his strength against him, and prove she was a force to be reckoned with.

Then Pinhead turned his eyes in her direction. Nothing more. And she realised this Pat Pinhead person was not someone you could best and walk away. He was someone you'd have to kill on your first attempt, or die trying.

He winked at her, and left the room, Veins and Basher trailing behind.

"Ursus urticant[4]," she muttered at his retreating back.

Lilly found a pair of boots in the cleaning cupboard. Clumsy yellow gumboots, two sizes too large, but good enough to keep her feet dry while sorting out the clean-up.

To get out of mopping, Brian said he knew how to operate the forklift. It didn't go well. The first thing he did was crash the machine into the Velociraptor cage. It roared and flapped its pint-sized wings.

The huge cage started to wobble, and Brian backed his machine up, almost right on top of the cage of an albino Burmese Python. A pregnant albino Burmese Python.

"Watch what you're doing," Lilly yelled, rescuing the python and jumping clear as the Velociraptor cage crashed to the ground.

The screeches of the very angry dinosaur echoed around the menagerie.

"Just getting used to these controls," Brian yelled cheerfully, spinning the machine in a tight circle and scooping the cage across the floor until it tipped upright. "I've got it now."

"You'd better," she yelled back, relieved the Velociraptor looked more angry than hurt. "For goodness sakes, these animals are treasures!"

The Velociraptor flicked a claw at her through the bars,

4 Ursus: a genus in the family Ursidae (bears). Urticant: producing itching or stinging. What Lilly meant by this nobody is sure. *LL*

failed, and then tried to swipe the forklift.

Once Brian got the hang of the controls, the job moved much faster. Soon all of the smaller insects and snakes were packed off to the safety of the lab next door, while the more delicate creatures had been partitioned off, using some of the larger cages covered with tarpaulins.

Three hours later, utterly exhausted, they sprayed the quarantined mammals, and mopped up for the last time. Lilly was almost too exhausted to stand, let alone think straight.

"I'm going to my room," she announced. I don't suppose any of you know where it might possibly be?"

"This way, Miss Lionheart," Missy said, ever so respectfully. Fortunately neither of the boys would recognise Missy's tone as being the type of respectful that is interchangeable with humouring the idiot boss, so Lilly chose to ignore it.

"You mustn't let yourself get upset," the girl advised as soon as they got out into the corridor.

"I'm doing my best," Lilly growled.

Missy took the hint and fell quiet, until she came to an intersection. "Um, our room's through here." She opened consecutive doors revealing a dorm-room with two beds, one each side.

"What?" Lilly demanded. "Surely I have a room to myself?"

Missy ignored her. "That bed's mine," she said pointing to the one on the left.

Except for a flowery bag in the middle of the bed on the left, both beds looked just the same – chilly and about as welcoming as a plank of wood with hospital corners. There were some lovely dresses hanging in the mini wardrobe on Missy's side.

Lilly sighed. "Fine. Please close the door on your way out."

She sank onto the bed and started pulling off the revolting yellow boots, and inspecting her ruined stockings.

Missy hovered in the door. "Don't you want dinner, miss?"

"I'm sorry, I'm not hungry," Lilly said, being about as polite as Missy was respectful. Although to give her credit, the girl was keeping up the facade rather well.

"I'll get you something, miss."

"You don't have to," Lilly said, but Missy had already gone.

She was half asleep when Missy barged in carrying two trays stacked on top of each other.

"That's very sweet of you," Lilly forced herself to sit up and smile. Chops, boiled cabbage, and potato. She put the meat to one side and picked at a potato.

"You never said how you got here," Missy said. "Did you apply for a pet-shop job too? Brian and I were so excited. We never thought we'd both get it."

"Oh." Lilly wasn't sure whether congratulations or commiserations were in order.

"So, did you apply too?" Missy asked.

"No." Lilly continued to pick at the inside of the potato. "I just ... got here." Was it worth mentioning she was a vegetarian? No, probably best left for another day. Instead, she yawned and put her tray aside. "I'm sorry, I'm too tired to eat." She collapsed back into her pillow.

A rustle under her ear made her freeze.

Carefully she felt under her pillow.

A note.

She turned over, pulling the covers over her head as if she just wanted to cut off the outside world and sleep.

"Great," she muttered.

"Are you okay?" Missy asked.

As if things weren't difficult enough, some idiot was trying to pass her secret notes. Missy? Best not to risk asking.

Best not to even look. Whoever it was probably meant to involve her in some ill-conceived spy-saboteur plot, the kind of endeavour that got people killed in a place like this.

Still, maybe the person contacting her knew what they were doing. Maybe they could help her escape?

Curiosity getting the better of her, Lilly tried to make out the faint writing in the dim light under her covers. In the end she figured out the words, *Are you Schrodinger's cat*[5]*?*

Nothing else, just those four words.

What did they mean? She remembered telling her parents it was obviously code for, *Are you in or are you out?* But apparently there were other things that could be read into that short phrase. Schrodinger's cat references tended to imply *Danger, Hope* and *Death*. Or utilised as a threat. *You live until we know which side you are on, so join our side, or else!*

Lilly smiled, remembering the dinner conversation not so long ago where Shrodinger's cat codes and their meanings had featured heavily. So, maybe, it was also a hint someone here knew her parents awfully well – or was in contact with them. And if this was a message from her parents, then they knew where she was. They could help her escape!

No. That made no sense. Even if they'd managed to track her to Mr Big's lair, getting a message to someone on the inside was a whole different story. They were good, but not that good.

Unless—

Her smile froze. What if they'd deliberately dropped her into this mess? Mr Big wasn't the biggest criminal mastermind in existence, and this could be considered a minor training mission – at least for her hallowed family. Couldn't they take no for an answer?

No. They'd never do that to her. They knew there were

5 A famous thought experiment where a hypothesised particle determines the life or death of a cat. *VF*

so many other things she wanted to accomplish. And taking up the family business to become a top international spy was not on that list. Besides, they needed her at home, looking after her animals, especially Embraldo, the lizard-gecko hybrid and Sharps, the toothed lorikeet. She missed them all like crazy.

Lilly took deep calming breaths, pulled the pillow over her head, and tossed and turned for a bit longer.

It didn't help.

Now all she could think of was how much her family would be missing her. Wondering how she was. Planning to get her back home safe to all the animals she had left behind.

"Shall I turn out the light?" Missy asked at last.

"Yes, please," Lilly replied. But that didn't help either.

At last she gave up on sleep, discreetly pulled an e-notebook from her purse and started writing under the covers.

§

Dear Diary,

The critters here are great, although they will need a lot of TLC after the neglect they've suffered. Given some time, I expect I'll get the staff and the lab up to standard.

My team seem nice enough, even though they are severely lacking in training. The equipment though, now some of that really is top of the line apparatus. Some of it's so cutting edge, I've only ever read about it in *New Scientist* and *Gene Splicing Weekly*.

Still, I'd like to know, how much danger I'm in? And when I can get some decent clothes? And some shoes? Walking around in yellow gumboots all the time is hardly the impression I like to make. I hope I can escape, or someone rescues me before my fashion sense completely dies.

I'm missing home. Sharps most of all.

## Internal emails: Dec 4

To: Flynn@MrBig.net.www.e
From: 3sftmSecurity@MrBig.net.www.e
Subject: LL
Time: Dec 4, 22:27

I am not seeing a code in her writing, maybe she thinks we cannot read her dairy as she carry's her notebook about on her person. Wait a minuet, she's hiding another piece of paper in her fist. Its a note—

Will report soon.

3sftm

§

Discreetly, Lilly tucked the diary away. She got up, found a napkin, flourished it in front of the camera, and started writing...

§

*Dear Minions,*

*I am awfully short of clothes, and a nice pair of shoes. Is there any way this could be rectified as quickly as possible.*

*Yours Sincerely,*
*Lilliana Lionheart*

§

•6•

# IN OR OUT?

**LILLY TOSSED AND TURNED** all night, worrying about the note she'd found under her pillow. Whoever had sent it might as well have asked, *Are you alive or are you dead*? And, if she was to be the cat in this equation, surely her best bet would be to get out of the box before it sealed.

If only she hadn't been so cocky when she'd seen that car. If only she'd run.

Quietly, so as not to disturb Missy, still lying fast asleep, Lilly crept out into the corridor. Nobody much seemed to be moving, not even any camera eyes. Heart in mouth, she took the opportunity to wander down toward where she believed the exit should be, softly drumming on the walls with her fingers. Listening for anything that might indicate a secret panel, or room.

As a minion approached Lilly tried to ignore her internal panic. *Wrong way, wrong way, go the other way!* But the minion, instead of marching her back to the lab or her room, sneered like she was beneath his notice. *Good*, she thought, and walked on. A camera eye passed her, floating eerily along like a jellyfish in the water. She pretended not to notice it as she continued down through the long corridor, until a glance behind confirmed it was gone.

She checked a door.

Locked.

And the next and the next. She tried not to think of what might happen if a door opened and someone was inside.

Ahead, the path split. To the right, she thought she could see the back of the kitchen. And to the left, lay the unknown. And an exit.

Lilly summoned up her courage by remembering Dr Deathless, with his crazy threat. " ... *if I die, I've wired this place to blow.*" It would be crazy to stay with a madman like that on the loose. Then, of course, there was Mr Big with his rabid Rottweiler.

She had to get out. The faster, the better.

Taking a deep breath, Lilly kept walking. The corridor remained deserted until a cleaner bustled past, mops and bucket in hand.

He went through a flash oak doorway to the room where Lilly had first met Mr Big.

Lilly tried to be calm. The door was open, just by a crack. Should she walk on past? Or should she take this opportunity? She drew closer, and stopped to listen. There was a slight humming noise, and the dull whine of a motor coming from the room, but no voices. Screwing up her courage, she took a deep breath and peeked in.

Something flew at her face.

Lilly rocked backward in fright as one of the floating cameras whirred past, pointing its creepy eye at her before squeezing through the crack between door and jamb.

Knowing she'd been well and truly caught where she shouldn't be, she started calling softly – not because she wanted to be found, but for the benefit of any listening devices on the camera. "Can anybody help? I think I've lost my way."

She continued along the corridor, trying to ignore the camera following behind with its dull whine. And there was another noise. Something like the hum of a refrigerator. It was getting stronger, along with a familiar cracking-popping noise – Annie? No, definitely not. Although it reminded her of the giant Rottweiler crunching on bones.

The camera eye raced ahead of her, as she moved toward the strange sound – a thin hum interspersed by crackling mini thunder-claps. It was close now. She could almost feel the vibrations coming from a cement-block corridor wall. What could it be? She tapped the wall.

Cement. Definitely. A door was up ahead, but she didn't get quite close enough to read the sign on it, before it opened and a guard intercepted her, his finger on the trigger of his stunner.

"Hello," she said, bright and innocent as if she'd met a friendly face on the street.

His face didn't twitch. "Young miss, you shouldn't be here."

"No, I'm meant to be in the lab. Is it that way?" Lilly didn't quite point to the door – that would have been plain unbelievably stupid – but just past it, as if the lab might be down the corridor a little further.

"Miss, you gotta go back the way you came. This here place is dangerous for someone like you. See through those holes, it's all electrified. We can't even turn it off from this side."

"Really?" Lilly said, with a ditzy toss of her head, wondering if she should cut the stupid act, and ask why – given a sturdy pair of shoes, or indeed her ugly yellow gumboots should insulate someone from an electric floor. She settled on, "What's the point? Why would anyone electrify a floor?" and used the man's momentary silence to peer through the gaps in the cement blocks. Lilly didn't need to fake her expression of confusion. There were guards, two of them, but that wasn't the strange part. Nor were the murder holes they hid behind. Well, they were an unusual design for arrows, but presumably perfectly appropriate for bullets to pass through. What was *really* odd were the epilepsy-inducing strobes of blue light, illuminating water misting down from pipes running along the ceiling. And the very annoying manual switch on the other side of the electrified metal. It had a huge red sign overhead. **Warning, Electrified Flaw, Manual Override.**

Lightning sparked erratically through sheets of falling water. The blue flashes and mini-thunderclaps were no doubt lethal. They'd require a bulky Faraday cage to avoid. Hard to manufacture one of those without being noticed.

So the electrification wasn't pointless over-complication easily foiled by a pair of rubber-soled shoes. Too bad the switch was on the other side. That made getting across difficult. She couldn't build a trank-gun combo to shoot the guards and the switch – breaking the casing wouldn't necessarily turn off the electricity. And there was no way to know if the switch was actually a ruse, or even a booby trap – the electrified system might be attached to a timer, or a remote control.

She frowned. It was a diabolically clever little system.

"I told you. Get out of here." The guard's hands tightened around his gun.

"Um, I think I must have got turned around. All these corridors look alike."

The guard smiled, but didn't move a muscle. "Well, you don't want to go that way, Miss. Because, besides the electric shock that'll fry you, I'd also have to shoot you. And I'd hate to do that. You are a girl after all."

"A girl? You know, I—" Lilly started. For once she thought

better of saying she hadn't noticed. Instead she tried to think of something a little less confrontational, and therefore less likely to get her shot. Before she could, alarms sounded. (And not just the ones in her head that said – time to go, this is a death trap.)

The guard encouraged Lilly to move on with a wave from the butt of his gun, but she was already moving, hands over her ears until she was just out of sight of the gun and could see what would happen next.

It was hard to think with the ringing noise slicing through her skull.

Half a dozen camera eyes swam down the corridor.

She scampered back, but the camera eyes didn't follow. Instead, they rose until they reached the speakers near the ceiling, and spun round and round, jostling each other for space, as if they couldn't get enough of the terrible sound of wailing sirens.

A heartbeat later the sound was cut and the camera eyes spread out in different directions. One headed for her, the other five toward the concrete wall, where the spitting noise was growing. Or was she getting her hearing back?

Yes, the sound was definitely getting louder.

Lilly let out a breath she hadn't realised she'd been holding, and peered up and down the junction as if wondering how to get back to the lab. In truth she was listening carefully as Pinhead, Veins, Basher, and Deva, the woman who had escorted Dr Deathless from their lab, emerged from the guard room.

"Crossing that floor is such a nightmare," Pinhead muttered loudly. "I'm always worried the boss is gunna flick the remote and fry us, just for fun."

"Don't even think about it," Deva growled.

Lilly stared at them like a hedgehog in headlights.

They walked up to her, four abreast. Deva's dragon tattoos rippled as the woman casually slapped Pinhead on the back, laughing loudly. "Lab-rat," she muttered as she shoved past. Pinhead sneered.

Lilly tried to tell herself it was good that they were just walking past. Better than the alternative. Only she hated feeling so small.

"Coulda done with backup," Basher grumbled. "They was tougher than I thought."

"Tell your boys to cheer up," Deva told Pinhead. "We're still alive. I think it's time to celebrate our good luck!"

"Sounds good to me," Pinhead said. "I'll shout since I killed five spies bare-handed."

"You might've killed five spies, but I caught the two important ones," Deva said.

Lilly angrily dusted herself off, trying her best to focus on what was important. Escaping. And definitely not thinking about all the things she'd like to yell at their retreating backs, as they argued about who'd had the most successful mission.

To escape, she needed to get past all the guards, cross an electrified floor (or turn it off on the other side), and last but not least, escape through the maze. A maze she'd only walked through once, blindfolded.

Of course she could do it – but only if she could find all the secret doorways. There must be an easier way.

Slowly mulling it over, she wandered around, pretending to be trying to find her bearings, but in fact looking for a room near Mr Big's. Someone as paranoid as a big crime boss would have built private escape hatches out of GKS, in case they were ever trapped in their own facility. It would make sense. Paranoia is the name of the game when everyone really is out to get you.

It would also be the best way to get to the annoyingly-placed switch.

She tapped the walls unsuccessfully for a while before Pinhead walked up to her. "Hey, lab rat, the lab is that way," he said, his face almost purple with barely suppressed rage. "Turn back. Go past your room, and it's three doors down from there. Understand? I'm on a break and I shouldn't have to look after the likes of you."

"Thank you," Lilly said, breathlessly batting her eyelashes and putting on her, *I'm so terribly confused* face. Partly because it gave her a moment to get a really good idea of her surroundings, but mostly because in her experience, acting dumb was a sure-fire way to get away with things. And people like Pinhead always expected so little.

Not that he noticed, he was fumbling with a tablet.

"Along this wall?" Lilly asked thinking she'd seen a seam in the wall that might denote a secret door. She gave the wall a quick knock. But, no, it sounded like all the other internal walls. Nothing special.

"Go on," Pinhead said. "Hurry up, and stop this nonsense. And get back to work, before Mr Big loses his patience properly."

"Sorry." Lilly flashed him a smile. "This way?" He nodded and she walked back to the lab, making a big show of counting the doors on the way, until she was sure he was out of sight.

In the end, she had two choices. Dead now or dead later. Sooner or later she would have to make a decision, but until then, there was nothing more comforting than a little uncertainty.

# •7•

# SNAKES, RATS AND SPIDER VENOM

A SMILE SNUCK ONTO LILLY'S face as she pushed through the lab doors.

"Squidge!" she said, surprised to see him, syringe in hand, already busy taking blood from a fat white constrictor with yellow spots down its sides. It curled around his hands as if trying to squeeze them to death.

"Hello, Miss Lionheart. Meet Esmeralda."

"What?" Lilly said. Then she noticed the name, *Esmeralda,* stamped on the cage's brass nameplate. "Oh, the pregnant snake I rescued yesterday. Awesome. So what other snake are we using for our snake-hybrid?"

Squidge looked at her quizzically. "Another snake, Miss Lionheart? But we only need one."

"Huh?" Lilly said. "Don't we need two snakes for a snake-hybrid? Maybe a nice venomous one?"

Squidge stared back at Lilly. "Yes, we do need venom. It would not be a snake-hybrid otherwise. At least not a good one. But I am planning to use spider-venom genes, because I always get bitten when I milk the snakes – and now I am a tiny bit allergic."

"What?" Lilly said, confused.

"Most likely I will die if I get bit by a snake again."

"No not that. Did you really just say we're just going to

grab the venom genes from a spider, like a black widow? And somehow we're supposed to put them into a venom-less snake? Yeah, that'll be a piece of cake."

"Good idea, Miss Lionheart. Black widow toxin is the perfect choice of venom. And we have plenty of antivenin if we need it."

"Good?" Lilly echoed. Really? *Squidge was taking her suggestion seriously?* "I did say black widow, didn't I?"

"Yes."

"I mean, you know, we could cure your allergy – it would be easier."

The boy didn't reply. As if he hadn't heard a word she'd said, he raced over to the menagerie and paced up and down the cages, loudly discussing the advantages of several creatures; a grumpy Komodo dragon, a fox, and a particularly garish pink and yellow pony, before finally pulling the biggest, most distempered lab-rat out of the rat cage.

Lilly shook her head. "A rat!? You've got to be joking! Why don't you just choose a squirrel? That's warm blooded too."

Squidge stood with the rat swinging by its tail. "Very clever, Miss Lionheart. Squirrels are bigger than rats. And they are much more active."

"Yeah," Lilly said. The horrible truth finally sinking in. When Squidge had agreed to a *simple snake-hybrid*, he hadn't meant combining the genes of two snakes at all.

"Wonderful." Lilly shook her head in disbelief. "Just what we need. A really active poisonous critter running about the lab."

Squidge, cheerfully immune to Lilly's sarcasm, nodded.

Then, as if to prove her point, the rat twisted around, climbed up its own tail – and bit Squidge.

"Ow!" he shrieked, shaking the rat from his hand. "That is the third time this month."

The rat, having dropped back into its cage, scrambled over all the other rats and stood up on its hind legs like a prize-fighter desperate to go one more round.

"Are you sure you know what you're doing?" Lilly asked.

"Yes," Squidge said. "I am helping you make a squirrel-snake hybrid with black widow venom. Nothing too difficult or dangerous. Wait a minute—"

She watched him log onto his laptop – automatically noting his password, *ATGCmagshn* as he typed it.

"I have already modelled the expected phenotype[6]," he said. He pressed one of the many Photoshop icons and turned the screen toward her to display a 3D model of a rather ugly snake-headed creature with patchy fur.

"And don't forget the rat, and the spider-venom," Lilly said.

"Nothing to it." Squidge didn't pause, not even with this level of sarcasm. Instead he rapidly began to type in a whole raft of adjustments. "We are only taking a few venom genes from the spider anyway. That hardly counts."

"A squirrel-rat-snake with spider-venom hybrid," Lilly said over the rattle of the keyboard. "That won't be difficult or dangerous at all."

"No, Miss Lionheart." Squidge beamed at her happily. "It will be fun."

"What—?" Lilly stopped mid protest. How had she managed to miss something so important? Squidge had a laptop in his hands. "Um, wait a minute, do you have email?" she asked hopefully.

"Do you want to send a message to Mr Big?"

"No. I meant external emails?"

Squidge shook his head. "Nobody has that."

"Sharefile? Bookface? LinkAlot? Any internet connection at all?" she asked hopefully.

He shook his head.

---

6 Phenotype: what a creature looks like – resulting from the interaction of the genotype (genetic code) and the environment. *LL*

"Oh. You think maybe we could make a router and—"

"It will not work, Miss Lionheart. There is no outside network here."

"But we could boost the signal—"

"It is difficult. The Boss is running a jamming signal, and a secure encrypted network within a well-insulated concrete bunker. Even if we did get a message out, what are you going to say? *Hey, I am a super-bright genius trapped in an evil villain's super-bunker. Come and rescue me.*"

"It might work," Lilly said defensively. "And besides, who said I wanted to be rescued?"

"One, everyone who comes here complains they want to be rescued. Two, I do not want to get caught breaking in again—"

*Breaking in again?*

"And three, I like it here. It is not so bad once you get used to it. So please, stop trying to get Mr Big angry, and get on with our work. You do not know how grumpy he gets when we do not make the creature he wants on time. People die. Besides, I want to make cool animals like the dreadbeast. If we make it in time for his spring collection I might be able to choose the next project.

"Wait, just a minute." Lilly finally realised that in all this talk of creating impossible creatures, she'd forgotten to follow up on something really important. "You said you didn't want to be caught breaking *in* again. You mean, you've escaped? How?"

"No," Squidge said. "Well yes, I did escape. But no, I will not tell you how, and no, I am never doing it again. And neither are you if I can help it."

"But ... " Lilly wheedled.

"Never," Squidge replied, and refused to talk to her for the rest of the day.

Lilly tried not to spend the day banging her head on the nearest lab bench. Squidge was sweet and bright, but he was no-marbles-left-crazy if he thought anyone could make that dreadbeast. Worse, the idea that two kids could make it, with only a little help from two assistants who'd never even seen a lab before – well, that made her suspect the boy hadn't just lost his marbles, he'd dropped them into a nuclear warhead, and fused them permanently.

§

To: MrBig@MrBig.net.www.e
From: Security@MrBig.net.www.e
Subject: LL
Time: Dec 6, 10:15

I pinpointed the note courier. 34txy. We holding him? Or closing him down? Also she lurks round places she shouldn't really be, and taps on walls. Perhaps, like it says in her diary, all she is trying to do is escape, but I don't like it.

3sftm

§

To: Security@MrBig.net.www.e
From: MrBig@MrBig.net.www.e
Subject: 34txy
Time: Dec 6, 10:44

Why don't you leave that 34txy to me. As for taping on walls, she can do that as much as she wants, its not like she's going to find an exit that easily.

Mr Big, your evil Boss and Overlord

## •8•

# DON'T PANIC

**SHEETS BUNCHED UP UNDER** her, Lilly woke in a cold sweat. She lay there, not wanting to move, as she remembered the terrible dream. She'd been stuck in an underground bunker with crazy people who wanted her to make impossible creatures. And in a hopeless effort to escape she'd been reduced to searching down corridors and knocking on walls, to try and find trap doors.

She tugged at her clothes. She was fully dressed, and wearing the exact same clothes as in the dream.

"Rabid Rodents," she cursed. It wasn't a dream. Worse, she'd only meant to fall asleep for a moment, to make up for her early morning wandering, and now it was half way through the afternoon. Two pm. Assuming the clock on her bedside was right.

"There you are." Missy burst in, all bright-eyed and bushy-tailed. "I let you sleep in, but don't you think you should be in the lab by now?"

Lilly opened her mouth, but couldn't think of anything to say. She grabbed an aspirin from her purse. Missy's chirpiness was making her head hurt.

"What's the matter?" You sick?"

Now that was a tricky question. Lilly felt her forehead.

No temperature. So beside her nightmares, and the actual living daymares of dangerous thugs and GKS laboratory corridors – and her desperate need to escape said thugs and corridors, and overly chirpy workmates, she was fine. She shook her head. "I'm fine."

"You sure?" Missy fussed. And kept on fussing, keeping up an upbeat babble until they reached the lab.

"You are late," Squidge said, barely looking up from recalibrating pipettes as they walked in the door.

"Thanks for stating the obvious," Lilly said. "What are you going to do, give me detention or something? That would be nice." True enough. Detention would feel like a holiday after this.

He ignored her sarcasm, or didn't notice it. "So what have you been up to?"

"I slept in," Lilly said.

Missy coughed. "Didn't come in till all hours last night."

Lilly glared at Missy. "I got a bit lost, is all."

"Wouldn't bother." Brian winked as if he was reading her mind. "We're sealed in like sardines here. I know, I tried to escape two days ago."

Missy smiled. "Why would you want to escape?" she asked. "Don't you like working with the animals?"

"Yeah, I like the animals," Lilly said.

"They're okay." Brian shrugged. "But really, I prefer cats."

Missy's frown deepened.

"And I like you guys too, of course," Lilly added quickly. "I just want to go shopping and see the sun, and maybe go to the beach, or the mall, you know."

"The beach is nice," Missy said dreamily, her smile returning. "I like the seagulls."

"So do I," Lilly lied. All the birds in the world, and this girl chose seagulls? Smelly, repulsive, noisy things. "Come on, let's get to work."

After three solid days of cleaning cages, and tinkering with the new equipment, Lilly began to feel penned in. Not to mention frumpy. The clothes she'd been given looked like they'd been bought from the clearance pile of a discount store.

In the lab, there was always too much work to do, and Squidge pontificating on whatever preposterous design development he'd set his sights on for the day. In the menagerie Brian was always trying to be helpful. Even in her room, there was no peace as Missy always seemed to be hovering nearby.

Determined to have a little catch-up time to herself, Lilly arrived at the lab just after six the next morning. She almost ran into Squidge, pacing up and down between the benches and the sink.

He turned as if to speak to her, then continued pacing.

"What's the matter, Squidge?" Lilly asked after the third circuit.

"Miss Lionheart, this test hybrid is taking too long. Mr Big will not like it."

"Missy and Brian and I have been busy cleaning up the mess in the Menagerie, but I have managed to figure out how most of this equipment works."

"Is that all? Miss Lionheart, you know it is not our job to be cleaning cages. That is why we have Brian and Missy."

Lilly bit her tongue – and spoke anyway. "If you or Prof had respected the animals a bit more, Prof might not have died."

"Here," Squidge said, ignoring her outburst. He pushed a hefty updated design spec across the table. A huge list of all the jobs yet to be completed was stapled to the top. "We need all this done by tomorrow."

"Seriously?" Lilly flicked through the document.

Squidge blinked owlishly.

"Tomorrow? Um, are you sure that is possible?"

His eyes blinked again, with raptor-ish intensity behind his glasses, and pushed his laptop into her hands. "Mr Big will kill—"

"Fine." Lilly said. "I'm onto it. I'm onto it. Don't worry, it'll be done."

"That is good. I really do not want to die."

Lilly rolled her eyes. "I said, okay. There's no need to panic."

"Yes, Miss Lionheart," Squidge said. "But I was not panicking." Tomorrow, if it is not done ... then we panic." He started loading the centrifuge with samples.

"Right." Lilly scanned the list of impossible things she was supposed to accomplish in one day.

*One step at a time,* she told herself, *and anything is possible.*

It was a lie.

And it was more of a lie when sometime after 10 am, Brian and Missy walked in the door. Late. She yelled at them. "Quick! I need you two on PCR."

Missy groaned.

"You'd think we'd get the day off," Brian said. "Isn't this the weekend or something? What's PCR anyway?"

"I don't care," Missy said. "We're supposed to be taking it easy."

"New plan. Sorry," Lilly said. "Squidge thinks it's important that we hurry. He was being rather dramatic about it. So how about I show you how the equipment works? Won't that be fun? You can get us some extra copies of useful DNA sequences."

Brian shrugged laconically. "I guess."

Lilly turned to Missy. "And you know, I did help you an awful lot with cleaning cages."

"Um. I'm no good with machines." Missy giggled a fake laugh, and hovered a metre away as if Lilly, or PCR machine, might bite.

Patience, Lilly told herself, taking care to explain everything slowly, and demonstrate the process from sample to result. "Looks easy," Brian said.

"So long as you're careful," Lilly warned. But to her surprise, he took to the work like a duck to water.

Missy though, could hardly be relied upon to hand the samples to Brian.

"Oops," Missy said, dropping a second tray of test-tubes to shatter on the ground. Casually, she checked her freshly manicured nails for signs of wear.

Was the girl even trying?

Exhausted by Missy's indomitable incompetence, Lilly decided to let Brian finish Missy's training. She couldn't hold their hands forever, and it was time for her to move on to mocking up the final chromosome sequences. The job took extreme patience and care. One mistake with a regulating sequence, or even a folding error, and the critter would likely kill itself with its own toxin.

*Focus*, she told herself, trying to ignore everything else.

"Look at this!" Squidge yelled, clapping his hands to his head.

Lilly jumped. "Squidge! I'm trying to do delicate work."

"But Miss Lionheart, this is terrible. The development of the venom sacs is all wrong! I am such an idiot."

"No, Squidge. What?" Lilly lowered her voice as one of the floating cameras cruised into the room, blinking its shutter on and off, disconcertingly like a disembodied eye. "Don't say another word."

She froze. This was bad. What if Mr Big got it into his head that someone in her team was incompetent? And even if he didn't, how were they going to get all this work done today, even without distractions?

Lilly took a deep breath, and stopped herself from telling Squidge to shut up. He probably just needed reassurance. She smiled. "I'm sure everything is fine."

He shoved the laptop at her face as the eye continued to whirr toward them. How much of what they'd said had been recorded?

Too late to worry about that now. She needed to keep on doing her best to make everyone look good.

Say something nice, she thought, scanning his calculations. Her eyes widened as she saw just how simple and elegant his work was. Pure brilliance. It made her forget that she was trying to do the impossible, it made her forget that her lab was carrying a worker that didn't in point of fact work. Say something nice, she told herself again, but she couldn't. If Squidge was as brilliant as this work indicated, then maybe the lab didn't need her after all. Mr Big could have her killed and it would hardly slow down his programme at all.

Aware of the camera floating nearer, she did the only thing she could. The only sensible thing. She sighed in aggravation to show just how stupid Squidge was to make such a basic mistake – whatever that mistake might have been, and reluctantly handed back his work. "Never mind, Squidge. You're still making great progress." It was a terrible understatement. His work on embryo development was a masterpiece – and it had only taken him two days! She just needed to tweak a few things here and there. After all, the creature he was planning to make was unbelievably ugly. But aside from that small point, she couldn't see any actual errors.

Squidge smiled ruefully as if he didn't deserve even that small amount of praise, and settled back to work.

Five minutes later – just as the camera eye was losing interest – he jumped off his lab stool, clapped his hands to his head, and proclaimed he was an idiot again. "Oh no, the venom-conducting tube is wrong too!"

"Focus!" Lilly yelled, dropping her own work to look him in the eye.

He glanced away.

"Squidge, you won't do this if you don't focus. Besides, you haven't even finalised the actual delivery method yet."

"What?"

"A way for the creature to inject the venom into its prey."

"Yes. Adjusting the salivary glands and surrounding tissue was a little trickier than I had thought, but I *am* almost up to the developmental folding of the teeth."

"You mean, for hollow teeth?" Missy asked. So she wasn't as silly as she acted.

Brian nodded. "Yep. So the venom can get through. Isn't that right?"

"Well done, you two," Lilly beamed, genuinely happy, until the camera floated right into the middle of the conversation. Was nothing around here private? "We'll make scientists of you yet." And if not, best not let the blasted camera know.

"Now Squidge, are you sure you're up to this? You've been nonstop for ages."

"Easy peasy. Natural selection happened by accident – how difficult can it be?"

Lilly nodded, and then shook her head. What was the boy saying? Replicating natural selection was easy? He was crazy. Still, there was no denying he was racing through work that would have taken experienced university staff months to complete. Years even.

His Prof might not have been the genius he'd proclaimed, but Squidge was almost as good at this as she was.

No. Best face the truth now – if only to herself. He was better than her. There was no way she could run this project successfully without him – let alone at breakneck speed. But maybe he couldn't do it without her either.

He kept on looking over to her, or more accurately just past her shoulder – but she'd already given him his computer back again. So what could he possibly need?

Oh. Right. Positive feedback. "Awesome, Squidge. It's great work. And don't worry about a couple of little mistakes. We have to expect some setbacks, even in a small project like this." *Small* was a lie, but it seemed like the right thing to say. She struggled not to laugh at the irony – not only was this the biggest project she'd ever worked on, but somehow she'd landed a job that relied on her near non-existent people skills.

By the afternoon, pain jagged down Lilly's back and her eyes ached from staring at all the data. Even so, she had to admit things could have gone worse, Brian was learning the finer points of running samples, and even Missy had lost some of her nervousness around the equipment. She also had an amazing knack of being on hand when needed, and remembering important details – like which drawer equipment could be found in, and when the animals needed feeding.

"I think it's time to quit for the day," Lilly said, no longer able to ignore her stomach protesting that it hadn't had a proper meal.

"You finished?" Squidge bounded across the lab to look at her work.

"Miss Lionheart!" he exclaimed.

Her empty stomach clenched in dread. What if he decided she wasn't good enough? What would happen then?

Squidge read the document without looking up. It seemed forever before he started gushing. "Gosh, it is brilliant work. Even better than Prof. Just wait." He tinkered for another half hour with Lilly's plans while Lilly, Brian and Missy all gazed nervously over his shoulder. Squidge repeated, "Just brilliant," for about the seventh time, as he made what was indeed a brilliant modification to the prototype she'd developed.

At last, to Lilly's relief, he pushed himself away from the table. "All done."

"Good." Lilly breathed a sigh of relief. "So long as you're happy. I'm ravenous."

They rushed out of the lab and down the corridor. "Watch out, lab rats," a minion said brushing past. The team ignored her, it was nothing new.

"Gosh, I'm literally starving," Brian said, his stomach gurgling loudly.

"Yeah, I'm so hungry, I could eat pudding," Missy said. "And I never eat pudding. It's bad for the figure."

"I'm so hungry, even rubbishy old potatoes and boiled cabbage is going to taste like pudding," Lilly said. She couldn't remember ever feeling so ravenous. Her mouth watered in anticipation, until she smelt something oddly metallic warring with the familiar boiled cabbage of the mess.

There was a slobbering crunching sound.

They reached the mess hall and stopped. One glance at the dog feeding on the two corpses askew on the floor and Lilly's appetite fled.

§

To: MrBig@MrBig.net.www.e
From: Lab2Squidge@MrBig.net.www.e
Subject: Miss L
Time: Dec 8, 09:12

You asked me to tell you how Miss Lionheart was fitting in. She is indeed an asset to the lab, a real genius. Our trial project is going very well.

Squidge

§

To: MrBig@MrBig.net.www.e
From: Lab2Staff@MrBig.net.www.e
Subject: Miss L
Time: Dec 8, 10:22

I do not like this new lady, she is pompous and overbearing, and she gives us all the work.

Missy

§

To: Flynn@MrBig.net.www.e
From: Untraceable
Subject: Urgent
Time: Dec 8, 10:42

Send the note: "Tiger, tiger burning bright—"

§

# •9•

# PANIC

LILLY TRIED NOT TO look at the blood and brains spattered along the wall.

Somewhere close by, a girl screamed. *Not me*, Lilly thought – slowly realising her jaw had dropped open. Her hand rose to cover her mouth. *Definitely not me.*

She looked about. It was Missy. A camera swam right up to the girl's face, but Missy ignored it and continued to scream over the crunching and snapping of Annie feeding.

"That's enough," Mr Big said emerging from the mess hall, a cigar clutched in pudgy fingers.

Missy burst into tears and ran past Pinhead, who was standing behind them, surveying the scene.

Mr Big didn't seem to care that Missy had gone, his eyes were locked on Lilly. His accusing tone ricocheting through her like a bullet. "That's what happens to spies, Miss Lionheart."

Too terrified to go forward, twice as terrified to move back, Lilly stood rooted to the spot, staring at the partially eviscerated bodies, the slavering dog, and Mr Big's evil smile.

She started to shake her head in denial when Squidge skirted past. He walked through the crowded mess hall, heading straight for the buffet and piling food onto his plate as if nothing unusual had happened. Brian looked at Mr Big's raised eyebrow and back at her before judiciously following Squidge.

Alone in the corridor, Lilly felt truly exposed. The two corpses seemed especially accusing. Who were they? "I'm not a spy," she whispered, wondering if Mr Big knew she'd been trained as a spy since she could walk.

Her teeth bit into the inside of her cheeks. What were her chances of surviving if she attacked him first?

Almost none. Not with Pinhead behind her. She took a deep breath. And with an irony that she swore she could taste – no, that was the blood from her cheek, she'd bitten it so hard – Lilly decided now would be a good time to use the spy training. *Whatever you do, don't stop. Don't stand out, and don't let yourself get upset.*

I can do that, she lied to herself. After all, she was already upset. Carefully placing one foot in front of the other, Lilly walked past Mr Big, and joined Brian and Squidge at the buffet. She heaped food onto her plate, and followed the boys to their usual spot, almost crashing into Dr Deathless.

"Oh look, it's dead minion walking," Deathless said, shouldering past her on the way to the whiteboard, where he loudly started a betting pool of exactly how much longer she was expected to live. "I reckon she'll live another thirty-five minutes. Max." Lilly pushed food around her plate and tried not to listen as the hall erupted in bets estimating her life expectancy in days and minutes. They were so engrossed, nobody seemed to notice Annie dragging away the first mauled carcass by his leg. Not even Mr Big who kept stuffing food into his mouth, and watching the room intently. There had to be some way of keeping out from under his radar.

After ten minutes, the dog came back for the second body. Annie growled as the torso caught on the doorframe, changed her grip to the other leg, and disappeared down the corridor – the last set of trailing hands leaving tracks of smeared blood in their wake.

Two minions rushed over to clean up the blood and gore, eliciting nervous applause. Soon after, the conversation began to approach normal levels. She listened for a while, hoping to find friends in this unfriendly place. But what she heard was a terribly depressing litany of how wonderful Mr Big was, and how terrible spies were – and who is this new person that has the boss so jumpy anyway?

Me? Lilly thought. I'm the person who has the boss jumpy? I've done nothing. I've hardly even had time to think about escaping, and he's killed two people I don't know to make a point? Why?

Ignoring the glare Lilly sent his way, Pinhead sidled over, and sat down next to her. "You don't seem very hungry, girl."

Swallowing her anger, she didn't bother trying for innocent. Stupid. *Always try for stupid.* That's what her grade one espionage teacher had always said. *The easily dazed and confused aren't often taken for spies. And if they are, not good ones.*

Why hadn't she listened more? Why hadn't she been thinking more like a spy.

"I'm sorry?" Lilly shoved her plate closer to Pinhead. She wasn't going to eat anything on it.

"You're going to be hungry later," he said sagely, and began cramming potatoes into his mouth.

Lilly smiled tightly. "I don't suppose there's anything less fatty around? We've had nothing but stodge for three days, and you know, a girl has to watch her weight."

Pinhead laughed. A deep throaty chuckle that sprayed chunks of potato everywhere. "The only weight I'd be watching is that pretty head that's currently attached to your shoulders. You're near as damn anorexic anyway."

Lilly flinched.

He grinned. "Girl, when I find out that you're the trouble I think you are, you'll wish you'd never been born."

"Too late," Lilly said. "Been there, done that. Already terribly disappointed. But you know what they say about wishes. Excuse me. It's been a somewhat tiring day." She looked hopefully toward the door. Big Mistake. From the head of his table, Dr Deathless caught her eye. "I heard the boss has a contract out on your parents. They should be dead any day now." A half grin played annoyingly across Dr Deathless' lips.

His crew clinked their glasses and smirked right at her.

"You're lying," Lilly said automatically. Deliberately not looking at Pinhead.

"Of course he's lying," Brian said into a growing quiet. "Mr Big would never—"

"And Mr Big tells you all his plans, I suppose?" Dr Deathless countered.

"No," Lilly said, keeping a tight rein on her emotions. "But … you're lying. You're just trying to upset me."

"Don't be ridiculous, everyone knows … "

"Not everyone," Lilly said. She knew she should be trying not to sound angry or upset in front of this crowd, but from the gleeful look on Pinhead's face she was managing both perfectly.

Pinhead got up and glowered at Dr Deathless, who smiled back guilelessly.

Mr Big finally spoke, to a sudden absolute silence. "Deathless, that mouth of yours will go too far one day. Anyway, you're wrong about that contract. Miss Lilliana needn't worry about her parents. They are perfectly safe … I mean they *will* be perfectly safe, so long as she does her work. As will the rest of her family."

Dr Deathless sat down, grumbling loudly.

Missy, recomposed after her earlier fright, walked through the door, into the middle of the charged atmosphere. The room seemed to rearrange itself around her. Faces smoothed, chairs faced their tables primly, and suddenly everything was back to normal. Or at least what passes for normal in an evil mastermind's bunker.

"You alright?" Missy asked Lilly. "You look a bit pale."

She nodded dumbly and bit her aching cheek again. "Deathless was just trying to upset me."

"You'll be alright," Missy repeated. "Just ignore him, he's crazy. It's this place, I guess. Had a funny turn myself just before. Don't know what came over me. A waking nightmare, or something. Strange. Never mind, you forget about Deathless, you hear?"

"Yeah." Lilly shrugged.

"Lilly?" Missy said, concern shining through her voice.

"I-I have to go," Lilly replied pushing her chair back and running from the room. Bad enough the deaths and the bullying, but human kindliness was more than she could take. She was so upset, she ran into the group of cleaning minions coming back from their grisly chore, and knocked a bucket of half-chewed human bones all over the floor. "Watch out, geek, or you'll be next," they sneered.

Lilly fled. As soon as she was safely alone in her room, she started to change for bed, meaning to put an end to the day once and for all.

Something rustled in her pocket.

*No*, she thought. Can't be. But it was definitely papery. As Missy wasn't around she pulled out the note and read it.

The script was almost illegible, like someone had written it in a cramped place in the dark. Even so, she recognised the line. *Tiger, tiger burning bright*. It was the first line from an old poem. A clue someone dangerous was watching her?

If so, it was hardly necessary. Mr Big had already intimated as much. Maybe it meant she wasn't being careful enough around the eye cameras. But she hadn't realised she was doing anything particularly suspicious. Until now. Now she would have to keep a special eye out for them. Even so, they couldn't be all-seeing. Someone was taking more risks than her, simply by passing her these notes.

Missy? Presumably not, they could talk in confidence any time. Pinhead? Maybe. He had been around both times. But it didn't seem likely. Squidge? Probably not, for all his brains he seemed to lack the ability to understand deception. Or someone else? A minion she'd brushed past in the corridor? One of the two people who'd died today? It was impossible to know.

Part of her thought she should be happy that someone was on her side – but truth was, this cloak and dagger stuff made her nervous. All night her heart thundered in her chest as she tried to sort through the implications. Was there a clue she'd missed? Are you Schrodinger's Cat? Alive or Dead. In or out. William Blake's poem though – with the Tyger spelt wrong. That could mean anything.

§

Tyger, Tyger, burning bright
In the forests of the night,
What immortal hand or eye
Could frame thy fearful symmetry?

In what distant deeps or skies
Burnt the fire of thine eyes?
On what wings dare he aspire?
What the hand dare seize the fire?

And what shoulder, & what art,
Could twist the sinews of thy heart?
And when thy heart began to beat,
What dread hand? & what dread feet?

What the hammer? what the chain?
In what furnace was thy brain?
What the anvil? what dread grasp
Dare its deadly terrors clasp?

When the stars threw down their spears
And water'd heaven with their tears,
Did he smile his work to see?
Did he who made the Lamb make thee?

Tyger, Tyger, burning bright
In the forests of the night,
What immortal hand or eye
Dare frame thy fearful symmetry?

§

Eyes watching. Stealth. Danger. With overtones that she was playing god. Was that a reprimand?

"How can I stop creating creatures, and how can I be in more danger than I already am?" she muttered at the unhelpful text, before diving into bed and hiding under the covers like she had when she was a little girl.

§

*Dear Diary,*

*I don't think I can handle this much longer. At least the lab is okay. Science is so much simpler than mind games and politics. My head is spinning. I don't know what to think except that somehow I have to escape this triple reinforced, well-guarded, concrete bunker.*

*Tomorrow when I am feeling less jittery I fully intend to come up with a plan to get out of here. And I don't need anybody else's help to do it.*

§

To: MrBig@MrBig.net.www.e
From: Security@MrBig.net.www.e
Subject: LL
Time: Dec 9, 00:57

I think from her dairy she got another note. Looks like we got the wrong people after all. Must say, I love her e-notebook, it makes our job very easy.

3sftm

§

To: Security@MrBig.net.www.e
From: MrBig@MrBig.net.www.e
Subject: 34txy
Time: Dec 9, 10:15

Or that its a major conspiracy with more than a hand full of people involved. Besides, she's cleverer than you think. Keep vigilante. You can't make an omelette without cracking eggs. And I can't be an international master-villain without breaking a few skulls.

Your Evil Overlord

# •10•

# HOPE

**THREE HECTIC DAYS LATER,** the snake-hybrid was fully coded. Its avatar, a strange creature with an eerie reptilian quality, stared out of Squidge's computer screen. It had large eyes, short legs, scales, a forked tongue and oversized fangs. Even the tail was snaky – the few tufts of fur tagging onto it looked as if somehow it had caught virtual mange.

"Urgh, that's ugly," Missy said.

Lilly frowned. "Yes, I'm not sure how accurate the picture is ... " She hadn't exactly been planning to create such an ill-proportioned creature. "I thought your first prototype was better. If we just switch back my original chromosome three ... " she extemporised, hoping the last minute change wouldn't ruin everything.

"It will do," Squidge said. "We are not being too fussy with this project."

Lilly raised an eyebrow – not that anyone took any notice. *What the heck*, she thought and made the change.

Squidge glared at her.

"I just want the creature to look nice – is that too much to ask?" More than that, she wanted it to be special. A companion. And it could be, if it worked at all.

"Waste of time," Squidge muttered.

"Good. We done?" Brian said. "I'm starving."

"One more thing," Lilly added the rshyb3 series organelles she'd last-minute tweaked to produce a social pheromone.

"Dinner was half an hour ago," Squidge said reprovingly. "There might be some left if I start now, so stop fussing, I need to concentrate." He switched on the video-feed from the microscope. It showed only fuzzy white – until the image resolved into the bottom of a petri dish. A moment later he placed several mouse eggs into the dish and collected a newly manufactured sample of snake-hybrid DNA. "This one looks good. Cross your fingers, here we go."

Lilly massaged her temples and tried to ignore her tension headache as she looked over Squidge's shoulder at the amplified egg on the computer screen.

"What are you *doing*?" Missy asked, jostling closer to get a better look. "Is this even going to work?"

"Shhh," Squidge hissed, continuing to peer down the microscope. "I am transferring the manufactured DNA. It is delicate work." He pushed the impossibly thin needle into the denucleated mouse nucleus, and injected the DNA.

"Shouldn't we make a few, and not just one? Check out how they all grow?" Lilly asked. "See if there's any variation? After all, it's not impossible this one could be a dud."

"What?" Missy said. "It *has* to live."

"No. Our other project is too important." Squidge slid the petrie dish into a special compartment in their new, top of the line, artificial womb. All white Plastech, with a high-resolution viewing monitor on one side. "This was just a short assessment of you, Lilly. Which you passed, by the way. So congratulations, boss. Tomorrow we will be ready for the real thing. I am so excited."

"Yay," Lilly said flatly. Trying to tell herself the embryo

they were incubating didn't really matter. That there was no point worrying about whether it lived, because it almost certainly wouldn't. No matter how much she had begun to hope.

Her main aim had to be to escape back home, out of this nightmare. So all she really needed to do was stall, and keep on stalling, until she thought of a plan that wasn't all hope and big fluffy fairy dust.

§

To: Lab2@MrBig.net.www.e
From: MrBig@MrBig.net.www.e
CC: HODSpecialProjects@MrBig.net.www.e
Subject: My Dreadbeast
Time: Dec 11, 14:15

Isn't it about time I saw sum results from this department? What have you bean doing? I thought Miss L and that boy were supposed to be geniuses. Get on with it.

I shouldn't kneed to remind any body about what happens when I'm waiting around during the New Year for a mascot that doesn't arrive. A result I would consider worse than last year when the second unit Lion-hawk pooped on Tarpin's shoulder, and I had to shoot Tarpin, the hawk, and the design crew. Stop mucking around on trial projects and GET TO WORK!!

Your Boss and Overlord
Mr Big

§

To: 11sftmSecurity@MrBig.net.www.e
From: MrBig@MrBig.net.www.e
Subject: LL
Time: Dec 11, 14:19

Remember, we got this girl for a reason. To find our leek. So where are all her contacts? Who is sending her all the notes? Why haven't you found them? Why in all hells is she writing a dairy? And WHY aren't you doing your job?

Your Boss and Overlord
Mr Big

§

To: MrBig@MrBig.net.www.e
From: 11sftmSecurity@MrBig.net.www.e
Subject: Security
Time: Dec 11, 14:27

I ashore you. Security is tight. There have been no more attempted massages. My survey lance says our initial information may have been correct. And she is a scientist not a spy. She knows her job better than the old Prof you had offed.

11sftm

§

## •11•

# THREATENED

THREE DAYS LATER, LILLY was still alive, and, to her surprise, so was the hybrid embryo. It all seemed to be going swimmingly well, until Missy started yelling.

"Lilly! Hurry!" She was hovering next to the hybrid's artificial womb.

Lilly looked up from a mile of dreadbeast sequencing. Her gut turning in circles. What could possibly be wrong now?

"Lilly, look how fast the baby's grown already."

"Not baby, foetus," Squidge corrected, without looking up from his computer.

"I think it moved!" Missy yelled.

"Really?" Interest piqued, Lilly pushed past Missy and peered into the tank. The creature, a tiny curled up pea inside its Plastech sleeve, wasn't doing much, but it was still alive, and that was a good thing. For now. Determined not to get her hopes up, she shrugged. "Wait until next week," she said. "That'll be when it dies."

Brian looked over to Squidge. "It's not going to die, is it?"

"Of course not," Squidge said. Still without looking up, he launched into an explanation about how his new and improved optimised embryonic conditions would let the embryo grow at an enormous rate.

Lilly didn't really believe him, he always seemed to be full of profoundly unjustified enthusiasm. "That's lovely," she said, gulped down two aspirin, and then thought about it, before downing another – for luck.

Maybe it was time to shift focus away from the hybrid. She forced a smile, as much for the camera hovering nearby as for her team. "Look everyone, whether this little critter lives or dies, let's just remember we're making wonderful progress with the dreadbeast. We should all be proud." It was true enough. They were doing well. Not only that, but even Missy was learning how to use some of the equipment. And Brian was learning how *not* to use the really expensive fragile things that were best left in the hands of Lilly or Squidge.

At least tinkering with the dreadbeast physiology was fun, and the models were good – brilliant, in fact. Even if, in the end, none of it had a hope of working. Except, maybe, for the all-important job of convincing Mr Big to let her live long enough for a brilliant escape plan to pan out. And for her to think up that brilliant escape plan in the first place. Until then, as head of the lab, it was her job to put the best face she could on this project. However impossible.

She was about to go for another exploratory walk when a familiar figure with wild hair, walk shorts, and an Hawaiian shirt burst into the lab.

"D— D— D— Doctor Deathless," Squidge gasped.

"Let me see this ... this nothing you think you've designed," Dr Deathless demanded. "I know you've got nothing. You kids couldn't even make a six legged mouse, let alone one of Prof's crazy creatures."

"But—" Squidge tried to interject.

Dr Deathless was having none of it. "Squidge, you're a fool! Prof was a fool, and now he's dead. You'll all be dead soon. Especially you, girl!" He glared at Lilly through straggly clumps of unkempt hair.

Lilly shrank back.

Dr Deathless loomed closer, still ranting, "You're on a fool's errand. You're making a *dead*-beast. Not a dreadbeast. It'll never work." With evident relish, he spat out all the reasons why. The breathing, the skeleton … all the problems Lilly had talked about on her first day. But the more he ranted that the dreadbeast would never work, the more Lilly was determined that it would. She even started to see some quite elegant fixes for some of the problems. Maybe she'd been working too hard on going through the motions of working, rather than being her usual resourceful self.

Even as Dr Deathless screamed and ranted, his rabid overreaction gave Lilly a kind of perverse optimism that they might have a real chance of making the dreadbeast. It had to be possible. Why else would Dr Deathless be so worried? For a moment (before she reminded herself she was supposed to be escaping), Lilly even hoped it could be completed in time for Mr Big's Spring Catalogue of Evil.

"And what have we here?" Dr Deathless laughed as he approached the artificial womb with the tiny hybrid inside.

It *was* moving. Lilly felt as if she was seeing the critter for the first time. It was so cute, a pea wrapped up in its own tail, legs gently flailing.

In solidarity she joined Missy, standing bravely in front of her creation.

"Um. Get away from that," Squidge shouted.

"Your creature will die. And then *you* will die—" Dr Deathless ranted.

"Get away!" Brian advanced on Dr Deathless.

More eyes floated into the room, diodes flashing.

"Yes," Squidge said. "The embryo is growing nicely. You should back off and get out of here."

"I don't much feel like it." In a show of clumsiness, Dr Deathless tripped over the spare artificial womb, so it smashed into very expensive pieces of Plastech and electronics.

"Sorry!" Dr Deathless said, turning to the cameras in a tone of artificial sincerity. He backed away with exaggerated care.

"Get out! Get out!" Squidge squealed. He raised his skinny arms like a boxer. "Get out of here," he repeated, this time with a conviction that belied his skinny frame.

"You and whose army?" Dr Deathless laughed, towering over the boy. He lunged toward Squidge.

Squidge backed off, eyes wide.

Coming to his rescue, Missy and Brian approached, fists raised just as unconvincingly. "That's right, get out!" Brian said.

"That it?" Dr Deathless grinned, unimpressed by this display of solidarity.

Lilly picked up a lab chair, and he finally backed away with an infuriating wink.

The door crashed open. Two security guards rushed in.

"About time," Lilly muttered under her breath.

The guards stepped aside.

Calm as a cucumber, Dr Deathless walked past them, stopped in the doorway. He turned and waved, a grin plastered over his face.

The last of her patience gone, Lilly threw the chair. It skidded across the polished floor and hit the rapidly closing door. She shook her head and turned toward the others. "How can they just let him get away with this?"

"Um, that would be because of his bomb," Missy said, gingerly picking up broken circuitry from the smashed artificial womb.

"Or the army of zombies he's promised Mr Big." Brian

picked up a smashed piece of Plastech and grimaced as black tubing fell out.

"A bomb, *and an army?*" Lilly whispered in horror.

"I do not see the problem," Squidge said. "I am pretty sure someone could disarm the bomb. It is only gelignite. And as for zombies, he only has two. So far. That is nothing, you wait. Soon, *we* will have dreadbeasts."

Lilly sighed. "But we'll only have one. Deathless destroyed our spare AW[7]."

Still, maybe that would give them a little more time. Surely Mr Big couldn't expect them to move quite so fast when the only artificial womb they had was already occupied. Could he?

"It might not be so bad." Squidge picked up pieces of shattered equipment, while the rest of the team looked on in hope.

Finally he shook his head. "Snakes bladders! What are we going to do now?"

§

To: Flynn@MrBig.net.www.e
From: Security@MrBig.net.www.e
Subject: LL
Time: Dec 14, 18:55

She's either very clever or very stupid. In either case she has made no effort to contact anybody outside her teem. As for her dairy – it seems to be just that. I'm not noticing any code. Perhaps she is foolish enough to think we cannot read said dairy. That, or she doesn't care. And it looks like you were right about her running around tapping on walls. According to her diary, all she's doing is trying to do is escape. Good luck with that.

---

7 Lilly[7a] likes to use this term for an artificial womb. *VF*

7a That's *Miss Lionheart* to you. *LL*

I promise I'm working on her security issues and will keep you informed – wait a minuet, she's hiding something in her fist. Now she's pushing it up to the screen – Its another note.-

§

*Please, can the people doing the washing around here read simple instructions like, "dry-clean only." They completely ruined my skirt. And don't you think it's about time I got my own email address so I can organise proper replacement clothing? My only vaguely respectable clothes are becoming rather shabby.*

*Sincerely,*
*Lilliana Lionheart*

§

To: MissLionheart@MrBig.net.www.e
From: DigitalSecurity@MrBig.net.wwe
CC: Lab2staff@MrBig.net.www.e
CC: HR@MrBig.net.www.e
Subject: Your note
Time: Dec 14, 19:14

Miss Lionheart you are now on the internal e-mail system.

As for extra clothing, please contact HR@MrBig.net.www.e

§

To: MissLionheart@MrBig.net.www.e
From: HR@MrBig.net.wwe
Subject: Clothing
Time: Dec 14, 19:19
Attachment: Minions 'R' Us Catalogue

Hi. I hope you have settled in well and are beginning to enjoy the lifestyle the WWOE offers. Digital Security mentioned you were after some new clothing. Well, they didn't so much mention it, as it came up on my search parameters. It's not like I snoop or anything. Forward planning is in my job description, and my algorithms were simply monitoring the digital traffic to create a more impactful service. As Lab HOD you may purchase up to 20 items in the *Mad about Science* range. Don't you love it? Came up with that myself.

Cheers,
*VF* Your virtual friend at HR

§

To: HR@MrBig.net.www.e
From: MissLionheart@MrBig.net.www.e
Subject: Your note
Time: Dec 14, 19:56

The selection of clothing is hideous, but I am desperate. So, if you could, please order the items I have chosen.

Fortunately a lab-coat hides a multitude of fashion faux pas, but I would appreciate it if next time you could find a more stylish mail order site than "Minions 'R' Us." Maybe it is because I am so short, but I find jumpsuits and bomb-proof overcoats lack a certain je ne sais quoi.

Sincerely,
Lilliana Lionheart

§

Annoyed, Lilly reached for her diary. How much longer could she live like this?

§

*Dear Diary,*

*No surprise the suits from Minions 'R' Us were hardly flattering. There has to be some way to get some decent clothes around here. Pity I don't have time to chase it up, when we're so busy in the lab.*

*Still, I have to keep reminding myself we are making great progress. Coding the dreadbeast from scratch would flummox a small army of first-rate technicians. And it doesn't help that a very expensive AW was destroyed by Dr Deathless. I do hope it's going to be replaced. And soon.*

*Nevertheless I have done my best. I've worked until I was falling asleep on my feet, with nightmares of spiders picking people up in their jaws, poisoning them, wrapping them up in DNA, and draining out every last bit of blood, until the spiders grew as big as horses – and just as unpleasant.*

*Of course, in reality I can only live in hope that our creatures will be that terrifying. For now, the biggest real-life nightmare is trying to partner spider and mammalian physiology. It's almost insurmountable – their blood is incompatible, their breathing is wrong, and their internal organs are completely different. On top of those difficulties, hundreds of minor, but delicate design modifications need to be made. For example the exoskeleton of a dreadbeast couldn't be the same as a spider's, or the sheer weight of the casing would crush the creature.*

*I guess we'll have to figure a way to design the chitin so it's a bit like avian bone, with a honeycomb of cavities. Structurally it's important to get that right first so the weight of the exoskeleton doesn't compromise strength. Even so, half of the advantage of making a dreadbeast is its armour.*

*I know every university professor I've ever met would say*

*it's impossible. And yet, with my amazing little team it just might work.*

*After all, the snake-hybrid embryo is still growing. And it's growing fast. That's proof, surely, that we know what we're doing. The equipment is functioning optimally. So, maybe it will take a little longer than some of us might hope, but success will happen, and soon. I know it. And I can't wait.*

§

To: 11sftmSecurity@MrBig.net.www.e
From: MrBig@MrBig.net.www.e
Subject: Where are my dreadbeasts?
Time: Dec 19, 21:33

Please tell LL and her lab that I am not a patient man. Make it very clear her lab is knot to waste my property on unsanctioned experiments.

Your Boss and Overlord
Mr Big

## •12•

# TWICE SHY

LILLY'S OBSESSION WITH WORK might have started out of spite toward Dr Deathless, but she soon became so engrossed, she found it difficult to think of anything else – and, if anything, Squidge was worse.

"It's all Dr Deathless' fault," Brian complained when he had to carry Squidge's meals to the lab for the second day in a row. "Couldn't you just have one meal in the cafeteria?"

"This way is better," Squidge said. "I like staying behind to protect the lab because I can focus on something important, instead of having to put up with lame dinner conversation."

"You don't mean us, do you?" asked Missy.

"Of course I—"

"Of course he doesn't," Lilly interrupted, before Squidge could say anything incriminating.

"Actually—"

"He meant some of the others." Lilly glared at Squidge, who as usual, failed to notice.

"I do not—"

"Come on, Missy." Lilly jumped up from her stool. "We'll go get some lunch, and Brian can stay here for a change."

It wasn't what Lilly wanted to do. She wanted to stick around and get the last niggly bit on chromosome six folding properly. But Brian wouldn't much like staying behind – and that was the point.

Almost every moment at lunch Lilly felt like running back to the lab, not just for her own work, but to see if Squidge was making a vital breakthrough. Even Missy babbled away about the embryo, and the research, and how exciting it all was.

"Why do you always wander around so much?" Missy asked on the way back from lunch, when Lilly made a half-step down one of her detours.

"I need the exercise," Lilly said, improvising. She'd been here for over two weeks, too long for anyone to believe she could get lost.

"Come on," Missy urged. "Let's go this way, it's quicker and I'm tired of carrying this tray. Besides, don't you want to see if Squidge has a new picture of the dreadbeast?"

"Sorry?" Lilly was distracted by two guards striding down her *long cut*. Were they heading to the room with the electrified floor? Or maybe to a different exit? There must be one. Besides, even if the thugs were about to do nothing more than bully someone – that would still be interesting to know.

"Lilly? Come on, let's get back to the lab," Missy repeated.

"You go back without me," Lilly suggested. She turned and began to follow the guards.

Missy hurried after her, and pulled on her sleeve. "I don't like to. Please come back with me. I know all the people here are volunteering for the animals, and it's a good cause, but some of them are scary."

"O-kay." Lilly took the tray from Missy, and before she knew it, she was hurrying back to the lab. She wanted to see where Squidge was up to with the new prototype, and, more importantly, if the snake-hybrid was moving in some new way. It had been doing so well, yawning and stretching its cute little limbs.

She couldn't help it, the creature was adorable. It had to survive. And if it did – would it be everything she hoped for?

Pre-occupied, Lilly almost ran into Pinhead and Basher.

"Watch it, lab-rats," Basher said, punching his palm with his fist as he walked by. "I heard you guys have been given the hard word. Wouldn't want you to run into any more trouble."

Lilly and Missy turned to each other. They didn't need to say anything. In that moment, Lilly knew Missy was as ready to protect her, as she was to protect Missy. The bullies moved on and the two girls beat a hasty retreat back to the lab. As they drew closer, loud chittering, squawking, and screeching could be heard from the creatures inside.

A lion in the menagerie roared as if to say, keep the noise down. And roared again. Lilly broke into a half-run, and hesitated.

Something was terribly wrong.

She took a deep breath, and flung the door open. Inside, the lab was the worse for wear. There were several broken stools, broken glassware – nothing too expensive, thank goodness. But she hardly needed a degree in calculus to realise there was going to be nothing left if this bullying continued much longer.

Squidge, sporting a freshly blackened eye, gingerly picked himself up off his stool. "Miss Lionheart, Missy. I have some bad news."

"Squidge! What leprotic larceny happened here?" Lilly asked. "Are you okay? Don't tell me it was that Deathless goon again."

"I am fine, but no, it was not Deathless." Squidge held his head as if he was worried it might fall off.

"It was Pinhead and his men. Did you not see them? They were just here. They said we have to hatch the hybrid now."

"What? No!" Lilly ran over to the artificial womb. It was

perfectly intact. "But Squidge, it's not ready to be born yet. It's probably weeks premature."

"The lungs seem mature enough," he said without looking up. "But it is hard to tell, the gestation has been very short."

"Far too short!" Lilly said. "You can't be serious?"

Squidge looked up with the lost expression of someone who doesn't understand why evil exists, or how to cope. "They said, if we do not get it out of his AW today, Mr Big will feed it to Annie. And he will be coming around later to make sure."

Lilly grimaced. "I'll jack up an incubator."

Squidge, his usual cheerful optimism stifled, began pacing the lab up and down, up and down … not really focused on anything, not even talking to himself.

Brian appeared from the office, a bandage wrapped round his hand. He seemed almost as dazed as the rest of them. "It can't be ready, can it? How can it be ready?" he kept muttering as he helped Lilly and Missy set up emergency equipment.

Lilly didn't blame him. She was asking herself the same questions as she grabbed some clean linen for the *birth*. This creature she'd helped design had to work – only it couldn't – it was impossible. Damn, she'd been so careful. She crossed her fingers, and wondered at the rush of emotion. When had she let her hopes get up so high?

"It's really happening?" Missy asked.

"Yes." Lilly set her jaw and grabbed a clean towel. "It's not like we have any choice." She nodded at a camera eye as it whirred past. It circled in a deliberate way, as if operating on more than the usual random noise-related settings.

Determined not to give way to fear, Lilly turned to Squidge. "I would advise against this option," she stated not so much for his benefit, but for the lurking cameras. "Still, if we are lucky and stay calm, we can still birth the snake-hybrid. You can do the honours and flick the switch."

Squidge frowned. “Silly. I know this experiment does not really matter – but I had hoped … ”

“Even if it isn’t quite ready – we do have a top of the line incubator standing by.” Lilly smiled. “Seems a waste not to use it.”

Missy glared at her flippant comment, but for once the sarcasm did seem to strike a chord with Squidge. “Yeah, right,” he said, blinking owlishly from behind his glasses.

“Go on. You do it, Brian,” he said at last.

They all held their collective breaths as Brian flicked the switch labelled, *birth*.

Nothing happened.

Realising she was getting a tension headache, Lilly took a deliberate breath and clutched the towelling tighter, as if it might squirm free.

They waited on edge as seconds stretched out to minutes. Lilly desperately wanted aspirin, but decided it was best not to juggle painkiller and a baby snake-hybrid.

Brian fidgeted nervously. “Um,” he said at last. “Squidge, did I do something wrong?”

“I do not think so.” Squidge tapped his foot to the beat of the monitor.

Missy frowned and turned to Lilly, eyebrow arched in consternation.

Lilly’s head throbbed. What if something was wrong? What if the chamber was malfunctioning and killing the embryo? What if … ? Her hand reached out to the machine. Part of her thought she might be able to flick a switch better than Brian. The more sensible part laughed and pulled her hand away. She needed to wait calmly. Her job was to be ready to catch the baby.

A slushing sound echoed around the lab. Something was finally happening.

"Phew," Brian dragged the back of his hand across his sweaty forehead as the artificial womb started heaving.

For a moment Lilly was horrified. What if the baby was crushed? No. Clever machine, it was clearing the infant's lungs as it slowly squeezed the tiny creature from the silicon womb.

An external panel slid open revealing an almost circular birth canal.

"Is that the head? Oh em gee! It is the head!" Missy exclaimed, as, streaked with brownish synthetic amnio fluid, the head crowned and slowly slid out, eyes squeezed tight shut. The rest of the body followed pretty fast. Lilly, almost caught off guard, just managed to grab the baby with the towel. "It's a boy!" she said proudly watching their creation take its first breath.

Squidge stared at her oddly.

"I mean ... I knew he was a boy," Lilly blathered turning red. "It's just one thing to know you're making a boy, and another to see him being born."

Missy squealed. "He's soo cute."

"Is he breathing?" Squidge asked.

Lilly nodded. "He's perfect."

"Well done," Brian said, clapping Squidge on the back. It wasn't very hard – but even so, poor Squidge nearly shot up into the air.

"Yes, well done everyone," Lilly said drying the newborn. She gently cleaned the critter. Brownish streaks of the synthetic amniotic fluid rubbed off on the white cotton cloth, revealing more and more soft downy fur. He had just a hint of a bushy tail, tufted ears and little yellow stripes down the sides of his body. Even prettier than she had imagined.

Missy oohed some more and said, "I can't believe he's part snake."

"Damn, you are right," Squidge muttered. "The morphology is not very much like my design at all." He shook his head. "Lilly, you should never have made that last minute change."

"But—" Lilly said. As far as she was concerned, the squirrel-snake hybrid was perfect.

"Never mind, Miss Lionheart. It may be useless, just like Dr Deathless said, but do not worry. It was a very hurried job, and it is alive. Besides, if I feed it to Esmeralda, the thing will not be a complete waste – Ezzy is eating for about twenty eggs."

Missy and Brian gasped. Not about Esmeralda's eggs, they already knew about those. What they couldn't believe, or at least what Lilly couldn't believe, was that Squidge thought he could throw their very cute designer critter into a snake cage.

"B-b-but," Brian and Missy stuttered as the squirrel-snake hybrid opened it's eyes for the first time, and looked up at them. Not the usual newborn steel grey, but a beautiful golden-almond colour. Lilly felt as if the creature's luminescent eyes were drinking her in.

"No. He has to go." Squidge tried to grab the squirrel-snake hybrid out of Lilly's arms.

Gorgeous eyes glittering from the overhead lights, the critter bared very snake-like fangs, and sank them into Squidge's hand.

"Quet-zeee!" Squidge shrieked.

"Yes, perfect!" Lilly shouted. "We'll call him Quetzee. Oh. Are you okay?" She turned to Squidge and saw that baby Quetzee didn't look like he was about to let go of Squidge's hand any time soon.

Squidge didn't say anything. He prised Quetzee's jaws apart with a practised one-handed move, and shoved the squirming bundle into Lilly's arms.

Quetzee turned around twice, before snuggling into Lilly's chest and falling asleep.

"Snakes bladders!" Squidge cursed, rustling through his fifth cabinet drawer. "Someone find the antivenin."

Poison? Of course, Quetzee was poisonous, how could she have forgotten that small detail? Lilly rushed to the fridge.

It took just a moment to grab the antivenin, but by the time she got back, Squidge had sliced his hand just below the puncture and was already sucking out the poison. Between mouthfuls he babbled, "This is great, now, for the dreadbeast, all we need is less squirrel and more everything else—"

"Um, should you—" Lilly wanted to ask if he thought sucking out venom was such a good idea, only Squidge wasn't listening.

"—more rat, more snake, and more spider. Especially all the web-making genes. Have you isolated them? You said you had."

Lilly hadn't quite, but she wasn't about to admit it. "How about gecko as well?" she asked facetiously as she handed him the vial. "You know, with gecko genes the dreadbeast will be able to climb walls along with everything else."

"Great idea," Squidge said. "I will get onto it. So long as you finish up with the web sequences today, and check the DNA superstructure we have so far. We have to try to get it into the AW tomorrow. Oh yes, and Brian and Missy, the AW needs cleaning and sterilising. The instructions are in the filing cabinet somewhere."

"We'll be fine," Lilly reassured him. Not because there was much of a chance they'd be fine, but because it was what he needed to hear.

She had the antivenin ready to inject when Mr Big and Pinhead barged in the door, a belligerent Annie snapping at their heels.

"Ow!" Squidge muttered as she plunged the needle into his arm a little more roughly than she'd meant.

"What in all hells do you think you're doing? My assistants came round earlier with very specific instructions!"

"Huh?" Lilly asked. "I was just—"

"You did tell them, didn't you?" Mr Big whispered to Pinhead so loudly everybody could hear.

"Yes, sir. We were very clear about it."

"Good. How's my dreadbeast going to scare away all the super-spies of the world if it's still hanging around in test tubes? "And what *is* that thing you've been wasting your time on?" he roared, swiping at Lilly, or more accurately, the creature now very awake and hissing in her arms.

Lilly pulled Quetzee away from danger, so all he could do was snarl, and bare his fangs in retaliation.

"That *thing* is ground breaking, it's a mammalian-snake hybrid," she said.

Squidge stood there. "I told them, I .... It is just an experimental prototype."

"And *I* am telling *you* that something *will* break if I don't get my dreadbeast soon," Mr Big said. "And that'll be you two. What did I say last time, Squidge? I said, *if it's cute, kill it!* I need a beast that will strike fear into the hearts of my enemies, not some fluff-ball," he ranted. "I need my dreadbeast. And I need it now!"

"We will have it in a week or so," Squidge said, looking more than a little pale as he stumbled back – away from Mr Big and the frothing dog.

"A week?" Lilly gasped. "Are you serious?"

"A week." Mr Big growled – as if cutting edge science should be completed in a matter of minutes.

Squidge shrugged, rocking backward. His hands clutched his stomach. "Maybe a little less if we start the gestation today."

"Umm," Lilly gulped.

Missy, her eyes stretched open to near breaking point couldn't have looked more terrified. She nudged Brian.

Brian, his face even paler than usual, turned to Lilly.

What was she supposed to do? This was a dangerous situation. And there was no point asking Squidge for help, he was turning a violent shade of green. His whole body shook in a reaction to Quetzee's venom – or maybe it was the anti-venin. Either way, it was bad.

"Sure, we can make the dreadbeast in a week." She shrugged in an effort to be casual. After all, better to live out the week, than die now. "That's why we were emptying the AW, because we're almost ready. But you have to realise the sterilisation cycle takes a while … "

"Whatever. Get your project finished by Christmas, or you'll all go the same place as Prof and Unit Two."

"B … but," Brian stuttered. "Seven days is—"

Mr Big gave them all one last withering look and stormed out, the door slapping backward and forward behind him.

A moment later, Squidge also raced out of the lab, hand over his mouth.

Lilly, Quetzee cradled in her arms, followed. She could hear Squidge retching as he ran to the toilet.

"Emetic exsanguination," Lilly swore, about to push in after him and make sure he was alright, when Brian barged past, Missy close behind.

"You guys okay?" she yelled after Brian and Missy.

Brian yelled something incomprehensible back.

"Good. I'm going to get on with the work. Call me if you need me."

Another garbled reply from Brian, but it didn't sound panicky. At least not as panicky as she was about not completing Mr Big's dreadbeast, and keeping her whole team alive. Their project was already so far from completion it wasn't funny.

Dammit, it was hard to think. What if Squidge was not alright? What if he died? Her gut turned. Her heart fluttered.

*Focus*, Lilly told herself. She took a deep breath as she walked through the lab doors. Somehow she needed to prioritise and get an embryo into the AW tomorrow. Maybe she could get something viable ready. Even without Squidge.

She had one week. One week to incubate a near impossible monster. Or escape an inescapable lair.

"I need Squidge. And I need him now," she said to nobody in particular.

"Prrrtssz?" Quetzee looked up at her. She smiled at him lying in her arms. Success. One impossible creature created – one absolutely unique and rather gorgeous creature. That had to count for something.

Didn't it?

Only problem was, somehow it didn't. Somehow she was in more danger than ever. And so were all her team. Especially Quetzee.

§

To: MrBig@MrBig.net.www.e
From: 11sftmSecurity@MrBig.net.www.e
Subject: Security Lab 2
Time: Dec 22, 15:42

We could have a problem in the Dreadbeast lab. Squidge has been injured. A bite of some kind. Without Squidge the hole Dreadbeast project could be a disaster.

3sftm

§

To: 11sftmSecurity@MrBig.net.www.e
From: MrBig@MrBig.net.www.e
CC: Security@MrBig.net.www.e
BCC: HODspecialprojects@MrBig.net.www.e
Subject: Lab 2
Time: Dec 22, 15:49

I know. So watt? Any more problems in that lab and I'll close it down. Then it wont much matter if Squidge's injured, will it? Because heel be dead.

I'm serious this time. Annie is getting tired of easy kills. My sharks are hungry. And the Spring Catalogue of Evil needs to be finalized in the new year. So I kneed that dreadbeast now, or I'll have to replace it with something else.

And don't think I wont hold you accountable as well.

Your Boss and Overlord
Mr Big

§

# PART II - TWICE POISONED

# •13•

# LAYING LOW

QUETZEE WAS SLEEPING PEACEFULLY, his nose nestled in Lilly's ear and no trouble to anyone, when Missy and Brian returned to the lab. A very pale Squidge trailed behind them.

"Miss Lionheart!" Brian said. "What are you doing? That creature is dangerous, you can't let it near you! Look what it did to Squidge."

Squidge mumbled something, and precariously propped himself on a lab stool.

"But he's so cute, and I'm sure he didn't mean to hurt Squidge," Missy said. She began to stroke the sleeping snake-hybrid. "Quetzee, did nasty Squidge frighten you?"

"Please don't," Lilly said. "He's trying to sleep. And I'm trying to work." But work proved impossible. Missy could hardly be dissuaded from annoying Quetzee, and anyway, Lilly was stuck on a DNA sequence that just wouldn't fold correctly. Unable to think straight, she decided the better part of valour would be to help Brian take Squidge to his room.

Propped up between Lilly and Brian, Squidge protested that he was fit to work. "I will be fine." He was still insisting as Brian heaved him onto his bed.

Squidge tried to get up again, but collapsed back onto his pillows. "Maybe I do need a quick lie down. Miss Lionheart, can you get that final chromosome finished by yourself?"

"No problem," Lilly lied. "Brian, you coming?"

"Shouldn't I stay?" Brian asked.

"No," Squidge said. "We need everyone working. Everyone who can."

"Are you sure?" Lilly asked. Squidge really didn't look so well.

"Of course. Besides, you need Brian's help. You can always get Missy to check on me later."

But when they got back to the lab, they found Missy sitting at the workbench in floods of tears.

"Come on, Missy," Lilly said, awkwardly patting the girl's back. "No slacking now, we've got work to do."

"But, Miss Lionheart," Missy blubbed. "The dreadbeast will need more than a week to hatch, and we've only just finished sequencing. And Mr Big said he doesn't even *want* Quetzee."

"There, there." Lilly tried not to sound as awkward as she felt. "Crying won't help, so let's get to work."

But Missy only blubbed harder, and Brian glared at Lilly as if *she* had said something wrong. "Don't worry, Missy," he said. "We'll find a way. Lilly is really clever with *things*. She'll think of a plan."

Great. No pressure then. "I think our best option is to work hard—" Fortunately, she couldn't see any camera eyes floating around, but she lowered her voice just in case. "We'll lay as low as we can, so Mr Big won't notice if we run a little late. Understand?"

Brian nodded in a show of bravery as a camera eye whirred into the room. It circled Missy like an evil mechanised jellyfish.

"Missy!" Lilly shouted, her patience frayed.

Quetzee woke, clawing Lilly's shoulders and chittering.

Another camera eye appeared. So much for laying low.

Lilly bit back her anger. They were all frightened, but if Missy wanted to keep her head, she needed calm down and get to work. They all did.

"Missy, come on and help us out. We're so close. We just need to finish up this last little bit of dreadbeast coding and we're ninety nine percent there."

If anything, Missy cried harder. Maybe the girl could sense it was a lie. Without Squidge, the work would likely take days, if not weeks. Perhaps distracting her was the best plan, and what better than a fuzzy little newborn?

"I know, Missy, why don't you look after Quetzee, while Brian and I get on with the final chromosome? Then maybe you can go check on Squidge."

Missy looked up. "Really? You think Quetzee's safe? You said not to touch him."

"He hasn't bitten *me*, has he? You were right, Squidge just gave him a fright, is all."

Missy smiled. "Squidge does seem to get bit a lot." She took a sleepy Quetzee into her arms. "You cute little darling, cutesy-cutesy-cutesy coo." Or some such inane nonsense. Lilly wasn't really listening. Surely Missy could do this one little job.

The newborn, even less impressed than Lilly, hissed, and all the animals in the lab went crazy.

"Shhh," Lilly said, rifling through her notes.

But Missy didn't take the hint, she kept on cooing and cuddling Quetzee as if he was a human baby – soft and pliable and helpless.

Being no such thing, Quetzee hissed again.

"Um, Missy," Lilly said. She looked up to see Quetzee lurch at Missy with his fangs.

Missy reeled back, and dropped him with a shriek.

Quetzee howled, and Missy staggered backward. Insects, snakes and the other caged creatures squealed and scratched at their cages, as if they were also trying to get away.

Spooked by the commotion, Quetzee bounded toward Lilly in a flash of fur, leapt onto her lab coat, and scampered up onto her shoulders. From this vantage, he turned and hissed at his tormentor – and at the whole world in general.

"Not cutesy, Quetzee," Lilly corrected Missy, trying to ignore the claws digging into her as Quetzee turned around and around on her shoulders. At last he curled up around the back of her neck, his cold nose on her shoulder, his long fluffy tail flicking into her nostril.

"Huh," Missy said dully. She looked down at her arm. Two tiny red spots, little more than grazes, studded her flesh. Quick as she'd been to drop the beast, she'd not been quick enough.

"Missy?!" Lilly reached out to help.

Missy flinched, staggered backward, and fell into Brian's arms.

"Sssss," the little troublemaker hissed, kneading Lilly's shoulders with his claws.

The door burst open, and Squidge, pale as a polar bear, entered shouting and gesticulating. "Eureka! I have it! All we need to do is—" He stopped and looked at Missy cradled in Brian's arms.

"What is going on here?" he asked, as Brian lurched, and dumped Missy onto a work-bench.

"Quick!" Lilly rummaged through her drawer for anti-venin[8]. "Grab that knife, Squidge, she's convulsing."

---

8 Antivenin is used to treat venomous bites and stings. It is usually made from the antibodies animals create after being injected with small amounts of the original poison.

Squidge paused, eyes wide, head tilted. "The knife has my blood on it, it might be contaminated. She might get AIDS or something."

"Do you have AIDS or something?" Lilly snapped back. Where were those blasted vials of antivenin?

"I might," Squidge said defensively, still frozen in the middle of the room while Missy continued to convulse. "Besides, I came back because I have work to do."

"Squidge, just find a blade! Now!" Lilly rushed to the fridges. Maybe the antivenin vials were amongst the poisons.

"Oh." Squidge pulled open a drawer filled with laboratory sharps. "I forgot we have spare scalpels."

"Useful to know." Lilly glanced at the large assortment of laboratory sharps. "Hopefully we won't ever need that hacksaw. Or those giant scissors."

Missy's feet rattled the metal bench top.

*Focus*, Lilly thought to herself. There, right in front of her was the antivenin. She grabbed it.

Brian, clearly outmatched, was trying to hold Missy steady. He leaned forward.

"Watch out!" Lilly said, as Brian and Missy's heads clashed with a sickening thud.

Dazed, Brian let go. Rushing to help, Lilly grabbed Missy's arm just in time to stop Missy thrashing all the way off the edge of the table. Between the two of them, they wrestled Missy back under control.

"Hurry, Squidge." Lilly said, fumbling the antivenin with one hand. "You need to make that cut. Without it, she's going to die."

Squidge moaned, a hollow sound. "I do not like touching other people," he said.

Lilly glared at him, and almost dropped the antivenin, before regaining control and plunging it into Missy's thigh.

Squidge didn't move, so Lilly glared some more, "I'll do worse – I'll get that Deathless guy in here if you don't do what I say, *now*."

A look of crumpled dismay crossed Squidge's face.

"Squidge," she hissed through gritted teeth. "Either cut, or help hold her down."

"No, no, no. I cannot," Squidge muttered. He was so pale, he looked about to faint.

"Yes, you can. You have to," Lilly said with false certainty, holding her breath as Squidge hesitated a moment longer.

He sliced just above the punctures. Blood spurted from the wound.

Missy croaked out a scream.

Squidge screamed too, but at a much higher pitch. Wide-eyed, he surveyed his blood-sprayed sleeve and side-stepped the growing puddle of blood on the floor.

"What are you *doing*?" Brian yelled over the racket. "Can't you be more careful?"

"Brian, he's saving her life," Lilly said in her best approximation of calm, ignoring Quetzee's forked tongue flicking past her ear.

Brian's eyes bulged, his face ashen. "Get away from Missy!"

It didn't make any sense. They were trying to save Missy. What was Brian's problem?

Quetzee dug in his claws into her shoulder, and, trilling happily, jumped right on top of the girl.

"Quick, catch it!" Brian said, but recoiled as, forked tongue flicking, Quetzee leapt past him and onto the floor.

Not that Brian had anything to worry about, Quetzee obviously wasn't attacking. Tummy almost brushing the ground, he was stalking the puddle of Missy's blood with slow deliberation. He completed a full circle around the red puddle, before slinking right up to it and sniffing.

Quetzee rocked back, snuffling. A bright-red droplet glistening on his nose. His long tongue flicked out, and the droplet disappeared. Then he dipped his head to the blood and began to lap in earnest.

"Get away!" Brian said. Having gained his nerve he began flapping his arms at Quetzee, leaving Lilly to try and hold a convulsing Missy by herself.

Quetzee hissed back, striking out at Brian with his long sinuous neck.

Brian squealed, even though it was only a warning. Quetzee hadn't even got close.

"Stop squealing, Brian! I need your help!" Lilly ordered. "Let Quetzee drink a little blood if he wants."

"How can you say that?" Brian backed away further.

"Because the only thing that matters right now is saving Missy. So help me, will you?" A trickle of sweat ran down Lilly's forehead.

"Is she going to be okay?"

"Sure," Squidge said, "she is just having a bit of an overreaction to the poison."

"Having a nice chat?" Lilly muttered through clenched teeth. The hint didn't seem to work. "I can't hold her much longer. I'm not strong enough."

As if to emphasise the point, Missy's hand crashed into Lilly's face.

"Oh. Sorry." Brian reached over to lend a hand as Missy's arm smashed into Lilly's face again.

Lilly tasted blood down the back of her throat. Red and white stars pulsed in her eyes. She was struggling to stay upright, so it took a moment to realise Missy's convulsions were slowing.

And kept on slowing.

Relief faded fast as the girl lay unmoving, her grey-white

face framed by loose twists of black hair, her breathing so shallow it was difficult to see.

Squidge didn't seem to have noticed, he was too busy grabbing bandages.

"Turgid tentacles," Lilly swore, rushing to grab artificial plasma from the med fridge. Not as good as real blood matched to blood type, but easy and convenient and better than saline.

Brian's panicked cries for help echoed around the lab.

She turned back.

Squidge was still bandaging Missy's arm, but Brian was bailed up in a corner with a very angry and determined Quetzee holding him at bay.

"We'll all need to keep the antidote close, in case Quetzee's poison's stronger than we thought," Lilly said, ignoring Brian's little drama.

"She could just be allergic," Squidge replied. "My bite did not seem so bad."

"Hopefully." Lilly stuffed a vial of antivenin into her pocket and threw one to Brian, who had finally found enough gumption to at least try and shoo the baby. "Hey, I don't suppose anyone would put this thing in a cage?" he asked, waving his arm in Quetzee's direction.

"What?!" Lilly demanded.

"Um. Nothing," Brian said. He seized the first thing he could find – Squidge's laptop – and waved it at Quetzee.

"Hey!" Squidge yelled. "Put that down."

Quetzee shrilled, and ran up Lilly's lab coat and onto her shoulders again. She winced, not wanting to think about how painful his sharp little claws would be when he put on some weight.

A bit of bandaging, a drip with more than enough pain-killer and muscle relaxants to drop someone twice Missy's size, (and quite a few complaints about the misuse of vital lab equipment on Squidge's part,) and it was time to wash up.

"Is there anything else we can do?" Brian asked.

"Live or die, we have done the best we can here," Squidge said over the running water.

"Of course," Lilly said. "She'd be better off in hospital."

Now there was a thought. After all the near death experiences, and rescuing people, she'd overlooked the obvious. Getting Missy properly cared for might just give them both the possibility of escape – if she hadn't missed that boat already.

Still, saving Missy had to be her first priority, so without stopping to think about how to best use this opportunity, Lilly yelled.

Several cameras swerved toward her, confirming her suspicions that the things were attuned to noise. It could be a nuisance. But not now. Now she was pleased to see them whirr closer.

Slowly, carefully, she spoke to whoever was observing at the other end. "Missy needs to be in a proper hospital as soon as possible."

She thought for a moment, grabbed a piece of paper, scribbled, *hospital*, and shoved it up close to the camera eye. "Please, it's critical, otherwise she might die."

The camera whirred and moved away.

"Blastocyst," Lilly said, and waited a moment. The camera seemed to be jiggling about more than usual, but no, it was nothing. "Binary blastocysts![9]"

The cameras weren't moving. Nobody was coming. If only she could convince someone important that Missy needed to be hospitalised.

She had to try.

---

9 A blastocyst is a very early stage of embryo, so binary blastocysts are potentially twins! *VF*

To: MrBig@MrBig.net.www.e
From: Security@MrBig.net.www.e
Subject: Lab 2 Menagerie
Time: Dec 22, 16:02

What is wrong with this teem? Looks like we are going to kneed another minion.

## •14•

# THE EXPERIMENT

BRIAN FUSSED OVER MISSY, mopping her brow with cold cloths, and asking Lilly to check and recheck her vitals.

Just wait," Lilly snapped at Brian as she rifled through the medicine cabinets and fridges to see if she could find something useful.

"But she's so pale," Brian said.

"She's always pale."

"And she's so hot."

"That's why you have the cold cloths. Just give me a moment, will you? There must be some way I can talk to someone," Lilly said. "Missy needs medical attention now. A real hospital. Her pulse is weak and crazy and we just don't have—"

"You could try the phone," Squidge said, not altogether hopefully. He didn't look that well himself. Pale as the inside of a potato, and propped up on a lab stool, keeping a firm hold on his laptop.

"We have a phone?" Brian yelled.

Squidge pointed at a red cabinet. "It just goes to reception."

"That'll do." Lilly pulled open the cabinet door.

Stuck to the inside was a yellowed sheet of paper that said, *dial 1 for reception*. The phone itself was even older. So old it had a rotary dial. She picked up the receiver, awkwardly put her finger into *1*, and turned the complaining mechanism.

As she waited, the ringtone loud in her ear, a hundred terrifying thoughts burrowed through her brain. *Would this work? Would Missy die? Could she hitch a ride under the trolley? Or?* It all seemed preposterous, but she couldn't give up, and not just for Missy's sake. The notion of escape beckoned like a five year old's dream of Disney World.

Lilly tried to calm herself by counting each ring of the phone. At fifteen Quetzee wrapped his tail firmly around her neck, settled down, and fell asleep again.

Squidge shook his head as if he knew better and wandered over to his computer, hopefully to get some work done.

At nineteen, a slight click stopped Lilly from giving up. Finally, a woman's voice crackled over the line. "Hello? Reception. Can I help you?"

"Emergency," Lilly said. "Lab Three. Patient requires immediate hospitalisation for toxic shock and complications from *Latrodectus*[10] venom."

Nothing.

"She needs help now!" Lilly demanded.

Squidge rolled his eyes and shook his head.

Never mind what he thought. This was Missy's best shot at surviving the night. Any other plans Lilly had for using the event to save her own life, were simply a bonus.

On the other end of the line the lady said, "Roger that. We'll get an evac team to take her to a hospital ASAP."

Lilly's heart beat faster. Missy would survive. Now she desperately needed to think. Contingencies and counter-contingencies warred in her head. *Could she hide on the trolley? Or use it as a distraction? There had to be some way to make the most of this opportunity to get across the electrified*

10 Latrodectus is the genus of spider black widows belong to. *VF*

*exit. Maybe they'd use a different exit?* She couldn't assume anything.

Laughter rang out over the phone. At least three minions practically bursting a gut, as well as the receptionist struggling to catch her breath. "You don't think everyone here hasn't already seen it on the security feeds? What do you think this is? A government job? You save her, or not. Mr Big won't give a toss either way."

"What are they saying?" Brian asked Lilly as she stood holding the receiver numbly to her ear. "Tell me!"

The person on the other end hung up.

Open mouthed, Lilly listened to the cold hard whine of an empty line, before slowly putting the phone down and turning to Brian. Her sudden hope dashed so quickly she felt as if she couldn't breathe.

Breathe out. Breathe in. "It's bad news," she told Brian, trying to let him down easy.

"Oh," Brian said.

"You know," Squidge grinned. "This is not all bad. At least your hybrid worked. And better than I ever thought."

"What?!" Brian threw up his arms in disgust. "That *thing* almost killed you *and* Missy!"

"Exactly! Quetzee has to be one of the most dangerous newborns in existence, and yet it looks just like a cuddly pet. Think of the possibilities. Miss Lionheart, are you listening?"

"Yes. Great news," Lilly said heavily. "No doubt Missy will be swinging from the chandeliers with excitement, if she doesn't die."

"We do not have any chandeliers – except for the one in the boss' office – oh—" Squidge stopped mid-sentence, finally realising something was wrong. "Are you still upset? I do not know why. You know, we should be celebrating. If Missy dies, that just proves your critter is a success. We can always get a new assistant. A better assistant. You know, she was pretty hopeless."

Brian glared at him. "You'll have to find *two* new assistants."

"Brian, no! They'd kill you!" Lilly objected.

Squidge shrugged. "No big loss. He is not much better."

Fists clenched, Brian approached Squidge. "You need to apologise, right now."

"Boys!" Lilly held up a hand. "Please stop worrying about Missy. We can only do our best to keep her alive, so stop fighting over her."

Squidge hesitated. "I thought I was clear—"

"No." Lilly glared at them both. "*I* am obviously the one who has not been clear, so let me explain. We're going to do everything we can for Missy because *we* are a team, and that's important. But Mr Big is important too. If he doesn't get what he wants, and soon, then we're *all* going to wish we were already dead. Understand?"

"So what's new?" Brian stalked away, slamming the door behind him. At least he tried to slam the swinging door, but it just clacked and swung back again, hitting him squarely on his bum. He yelped indignantly and stormed off.

"He'll be back," Lilly said.

Squidge wasn't listening – he'd had taken up Prof's old sketchbook and was doodling in the margin.

"Prrrtssz." A claw poked into Lilly's neck and Quetzee's forked tongue flicked in and out disconcertingly near her cheek.

"Quetzee, stop it."

Chittering plaintively, Quetzee jumped down onto a lab bench, slowly picking his way toward Missy.

The other animals rustled, keeping a wary eye on this newcomer, who yowled plaintively.

"You stay out of trouble, you hear?" Lilly scooped up the little ball of fur.

"You think Missy is going to die?" Squidge asked conversationally.

"Might," Lilly replied. "Still, she's stable for now, and that's a good sign. But you'll have to look after her for a bit. Do you think you're up to it? It's just that I've got a baby here – and he's quite hungry."

"Okay. If you insist," Squidge said, barely looking up from the sketchbook.

Lilly rushed off to grab pre-mix kitten formula from the fridge, and a bottle from the steriliser[11]. She settled into a chair where she could keep an eye on Squidge and Melissa while she fed Quetzee.

It was a messy operation. Quetzee sicked up almost as much milk as he sucked down. Sometime in the middle of it all, Brian crept back into the lab, and began working on completing his sequencing job. He looked, if anything, more jumpy than when he'd left.

"I fail to see why everyone is so upset," Squidge said. "Lilly, that Quetzee of yours is a right terror. *And* you had that brilliant idea of adding gecko genes to the dreadbeasts. We are making great progress. Might even be ready to incubate in a couple of days."

"What?" Brian said, glaring at Squidge and rubbing his arm. "Don't you care about Missy? Or the fact that our lives are on the line?" He drew his finger dramatically across his throat.

Squidge shrugged. "Haste makes waste. What we are doing here is ground breaking."

"Squidge, Lilly, please. I think they really meant it. Melissa was so worried."

"I guess if we work through the night, we could get everything wrapped up," Squidge said with his usual interminable optimism. So long as you have isolated those gecko

11 An ultra clean dishwasher for laboratories, every parental unit should have one.

genes and integrated them into the final chromosome."

"Yes, Squidge," Lilly rolled her eyes. "It was the gecko genes I was really worried about. "You want flying on that chromosome as well?"

He nodded and then shook his head. "Not flying. Not yet anyway. Maybe later we will attempt a flying prototype. Still, even without wings, the new dreadbeast will be pretty exciting."

"I thought almost killing Missy was more than enough excitement," Brian muttered, "without us trying to get ourselves all killed as well."

Lilly sighed. "Fine Brian, we've got the message. But we can only do our best. Understand?"

"Talking about our best," Squidge said. "Lilly, do you have the gecko genes ready or not?"

"Couldn't you help?" Lilly asked. There were some other tweaks she needed to do if she wanted the creature to respond to social cues. If she got it right, the dreadbeasts might even team up with Quetzee.

"No," Squidge said. "Not yet anyway. I need to run my simulations to make sure we are on track. You cannot rush cutting edge science. I mean that cute thing we made is great, but it is not nearly so advanced as our dreadbeasts."

"This is going to take forever," Brian groaned.

"Not forever," Squidge said thoughtfully. "We are taking care because Mr Big wants something worthy of our genius. And so do I. Just think, if we get the dreadbeast right, and we should, we will be at the forefront of mutant animal engineering. The head billing on *The Spring Catalogue of Evil.*"

"I'm sure that's going to make this all worthwhile," Brian said, looking over to Missy.

"Yes," Squidge replied, beaming happily.

To: MrBig@MrBig.net.www.e
From: Security@MrBig.net.www.e
Subject: Lab 2
Time: Dec 22, 17:11

The minion problem seems to be sorted.

§

To: Security@MrBig.net.www.e
From: MrBig@MrBig.net.www.e
Subject: Lab 2
Time: Dec 22, 17:22

Can you believe them, trying to fob that pathetic creature of on me when I asked for a Dreadbeast?

Your Boss and Overlord
Mr Big

§

To: MrBig@MrBig.net.www.e
From: Security@MrBig.net.www.e
Subject: Lab 2
Time: Dec 22, 17:26

Cheer up, that 'pathetic creature' might be more useful than you thought. And more dangerous. It will be interesting to see who else is bitten.

# •15•

# QUETZEE

QUETZEE GRASPED THE BOTTLE in his paws, sucking the life out of it – until his little teeth punctured the nipple, and milk oozed down his front.

He chittered unhappily.

"Serves you right you greedy thing," Lilly murmured carefully wiping him down with a hand cloth. After he was clean and dry, he puked a couple more times.

Lilly cleaned him down each time, and tossed the cloths into the growing pile of washing. ".

Tummy distended, he finally crawled up onto Lilly's shoulders like an over-fed baby possum and fell asleep. As she passed through the lab on the way to dinner, Brian was sitting next to Melissa's bed. "How is she?" Lilly asked.

"Quiet," Brian said.

The readings on the monitors confirmed Missy was stable, and sleeping soundly.

"Well done, Brian. I think we're out of the woods," Lilly said, reducing the painkiller and introducing a small dose of sedative. "You coming to dinner?"

"I think I'll stay here."

"Your call." Lilly headed out into the corridor. As an afterthought she turned around. "How about I bring you back something?"

"That'll be nice, thanks." Brian flashed a lop-sided grin.

"No problem." Lilly rushed out the door – and almost collided with a small group of minions.

Quetzee woke as Lilly dodged aside. He dug in his claws and hissed.

A burly thug tripped over in his scramble to get away. Then, even stranger, he didn't curse her, threaten her, or even tell her to watch out. Neither did his two companions.

That was odd.

Caution being the better part of valour, Lilly gave them plenty of room to make their escape.

The next group she passed was larger. Thugs mostly, and a couple of techies. One of the techies loudly whispered something about venomous creatures to his friends as they slunk past, going out of their way to avoid her.

News of Missy's bite must have done the rounds – and maybe grown in the telling. Lilly blushed. "It was my fault, Quetzee, not yours," she whispered to the small creature on her shoulder. "I should've looked after you better. Anyway, Missy will be alright. Brian is looking after her."

She blushed even harder when she heard a little snore and realised she was not only talking to a baby animal, but one who had already fallen fast asleep again.

Desperate to get to the dinner hall before it closed, she almost ran into Deva, the heavily muscled guard who had corralled Dr Deathless on her first day.

"Get the – !" Deva started to yell, before turning white, and taking a ponderous step backward. Without another word, Deva turned and headed off in the other direction, shaking her head as if she'd forgotten something important. (Possibly that she was carrying twice as much weight, and infinite times as many guns as Lilly.)

Lilly grinned. Maybe this was a good thing. She didn't have to feel scared, or embarrassed. She was no longer yet another bullied minion for the WWWOE's vast evil enterprise. Now she was, if not important, someone who mattered. Someone who could do what she wanted and not be picked on by everyone who wanted to make her feel she was less important than them.

Lilly thought about exploring the boundary again and trying to escape. Only things were just getting interesting. Besides she ought to stay a little longer. She owed Missy that much.

As she entered the mess with its disturbingly familiar smell of boiled cabbage, Dr Deathless looked up.

What now? But he didn't say anything. He looked back down at his food. No sneering. In fact the whole room was hushed, conversations subsiding to whispers before returning a nervously shrill full volume.

Quetzee woke, clawing her shoulders as he turned round and round. It made her search for salad (on the off chance that she might live long enough to die of scurvy) quite a mission. No parsley, nothing. Cursing that this was a dreadful way to run an underground bunker, she began loading plates for the whole lab with the only two meatless options available – fried cabbage and mashed potatoes.

While she was balancing her tower of plates, Quetzee jumped off her shoulder and ran up and down the serving table.

Nobody complained. Not loudly anyway, but the whispers did get louder when he hooked some bacon on his claw and started gnawing on it.

"Shoulders, Quetzee," she ordered.

He didn't move, so she picked him up, put him back on

her shoulders, and rushed back to the lab with the carefully stacked tray of plates. Not that anyone seemed to care. Missy was still fast asleep from the sedative, and the others weren't that enthused about food either. Not even Brian.

They probably need cheering up, Lilly thought, looking around at the gloomy faces. So she told them the story of how Quetzee had jumped up on the table. Even embellished it a little, by saying he'd stolen food from Doctor Deathless' plate.

"Nice," Squidge said with a half-smile.

"Yeah, wonderful." Brian frowned and picked some batter off his fried cabbage. Lilly didn't blame him, the cooks here were dreadful. While they were still pushing food around their plates, Squidge jumped up and declared it was time to get back to work.

Lilly sighed. He was right. She was not only behind with the coding, but if she wasn't careful the menagerie would slip back to its former condition. "Um, Brian, with all this lab work, I haven't had time to clean any cages."

Brian didn't move.

"I could keep an eye on Missy and finish up this dreadbeast work. You know, before Mr Big decides to kill all of us?" she prompted, hoping the threat of death would motivate him. After all, he'd seemed very worried about dying earlier in the day.

Brian grunted something about only the dreadbeasts mattering. But he didn't budge, fussing over Missy, as if she was about to do something interesting.

"There's never a good enough excuse to leave critters in poor condition," Lilly muttered.

Except tonight. Tonight she was on a deadline. Squidge helped, juggling his projects alongside hers, so the work went faster than she might have hoped. Mostly. Because every time she thought she was finished, Squidge would find one more thing that needed to be done. Or should be done. Or he just wanted to do because it would be *awesome*.

After three in the morning, she dragged herself to bed, leaving Squidge to complete the finishing touches on a batch of six zygotes[12].

His determination that the dreadbeast embryo they chose to put in the AW[13] would be perfect, was so different from when they'd coded Quetzee, that Lilly didn't know whether to be surprised or worried.

Lilly threw herself onto her bed, fully dressed, and tried very hard not to think about Missy's empty bed on the other side. Then she tried even harder not to think about the dreadbeasts. Or Mr Big's retribution if the creatures failed to thrive. Had Squidge managed to get them into the incubator – or was he still fussing?

Only when she closed her eyes did she realise the light was still on. "Damn. Oh, Quetzee, turn off the light, will you?" Of course he didn't. But surely he could? Lilly dragged herself out of bed and slapped the switch with her hand. "Quetzee – Lights."

Quetzee rolled onto his back, waving his paws in the air and flicking his tail from side to side.

It was a simple task, and he was bright enough, but maybe he needed a little incentive. Food.

The idea gripped her. If she wasn't wondering if Quetzee could be trained to do this one simple job, she was worrying about Missy. And Squidge. Had he finished the dreadbeast like he'd promised? Giving up on sleep, Lilly pushed aside

12 Zygote – the earliest developmental stage of an embryo. *LL*

13 Artificial Womb – another thing all parental units should have (and absolutely indispensable for expectant fathers). *VF*

her exhaustion, put Quetzee up onto her shoulders, and rushed to the kitchen for some bacon.

Taking the bacon wasn't as difficult a task as it might have been. One of the night chefs did try and hit her over the head with a rolling pin, but he retreated as soon as Quetzee hissed and flicked out his forked tongue.

Then, one last detour to check on Squidge and Missy.

On the way, Quetzee climbed down her jacket and stuck his nose in her pocket looking for the bacon. His teeth bit into the plastic container, and he chittered angrily.

"Hold on." Lilly pulled him away.

He nosed back again, so she held the pocket closed with her hand and pushed through into the lab

Inside was the reassuring ping of Missy's monitor. Brian was half asleep on a lab-stool, hovering near the sleeping Missy, and a very pale Squidge still hunched over his laptop.

"Um, you finished?" she asked, noticing a tray of perishable ampoules abandoned on the bench. Typical. It was lucky she came back to check.

"You know how you mentioned flying the other day? I was just having a think."

"No," Lilly said. "You need to finish up."

"But it will not be that difficult. One more day. That is all. Imagine our dreadbeasts flying through the corridors."

Lilly wasn't sure she wanted to imagine that. Not unless she knew she could control them. Otherwise flying dreadbeasts would be far too dangerous.

"Can you pull up the original? *Before* you started tinkering with flying."

Squidge shrugged his shoulders and pulled up *Dreadbeast Mark 17.5*. Red warnings flashed ominously in the corner of the prototype screen.

"That doesn't look ready. Squidge, you said it was ready.

"What's the matter?"

"I ran the pre-check and the program does not appear to like the cold and warm blooded cross."

"Is that all?"

"I am not sure," Squidge admitted. "But it does disappear when I change the temperature parameters."

Lilly sighed. "Is that why you were playing with flight?"

"I thought it might help."

Lilly found herself seriously considering flight as an option. Only it was crazy. There would be a whole host of new difficulties and a far greater chance of failing. "No, flight's only going to make everything more difficult. We'll have to go with what we've got."

Worried Squidge might get distracted again, Lilly decided to stay and help. She looked around his workbench, something was off. What was he up to? She grabbed the ampoules and checked the labels. "These are not the same plasmids[14] and mitochondria we used for Quetzee."

"I thought we would use different ones. Stick to those found in spiders and snakes."

"No. I think we should throw in the same plasmids and mitochondria[15] we used for Quetzee."

"All of them? Squidge asked. "Including the rshyb3 series?"

"Especially the rshyb3 series," Lilly said.

"But half the genes on those seem to be some kind of social pheromone. Did you add it?"

"Of course I did," Lilly said. "I want creatures capable of working together."

Squidge sighed. "Fine. But if you liked it so much, you should have put it on the chromosomes proper."

---

14 Plasmids are small, circular, double stranded DNA molecules. *VF*

15 Mitochondria – often called the power houses of the cell, provide energy for the cell using a process called glycolysis to turn simple sugars into ATP (adenosine triphosphate) . *VF*

"Yes. Um," Lilly thought quickly. No need to tell him it was a seat of the pants decision. "But, you know, if our creatures are going to be used to attack other facilities, we might not need them all to be social."

"Ah," Squidge said. "Very clever. Here we are – cross your fingers."

Lilly held her breath, and though it was a silly superstition, crossed her fingers, as one by one he injected three mouse eggs and placed their petrie dish into the incubator.

"Tomorrow, can I choose which one to put into the AW?" Squidge asked.

"Sure," Lilly replied, feeling generous. "Congratulations, now go to bed."

Squidge grumbled something about not sleeping and shuffled off. It all felt horribly flat. The embryos had been created. They should've been celebrating. But Lilly couldn't rid herself of the lingering doubt they might not be viable. The temperature warning flashing on the design programme was a worry. Still, Squidge had pulled off miracles before... and in any case, they wouldn't have to worry about imminent death – for at least a day or two.

Now that was over, it was time for a little scientific enquiry. Could Quetzee be trained? She checked her pocket for the bacon. It was still there.

Quetzee prrrted from her shoulder, and, as if on cue, made yet another foray for the bacon.

"Yes, yes, soon," she reassured him. Hurrying to get to her room and close the door on the outside world.

Lilly opened the container. As the smell of bacon wafted out, Quetzee he ran down her arm in excitement, his tiny claws biting into her bare skin.

"Lights," she said, putting a piece of bacon on the switch.

Quetzee reached over and bashed at the bacon with his paw – the light turned off – and Quetzee hissed and scampered back up her arm.

"Good boy," Lilly said, ignoring the pain and calmly breaking off another piece of bacon. She repeated the experiment until Quetzee no longer needed bacon over the switch, but only the command, "Lights." Once, twice, three times his little paw bashed the switch in response to her command, and she rewarded him every time. With the light properly subdued, Lilly gave him the last piece of bacon and fell into bed.

After licking the empty bacon container, he jumped onto the bed and curled up on top of the covers, purring away like an expensive car.

§

*Dear Diary,*

*Quetzee is dangerous, so that's success. Apparently it's not enough. Mr Big wants nasty dangerous critters to put the fear of death and dismemberment into his enemies. Still, I've been wondering if Quetzee could be more than randomly dangerous. Could he be trained? Could he be given simple instructions and carry them out?*

*What could Quetzee do that will make him even more useful to Mr Big?*

*I'm sure with his skill set he could become indispensable. Not in my wildest dreams did I think we would ever make anything so awesome – and on our first go too.*

§

To: Security@MrBig.net.www.e
From: MrBig@MrBig.net.www.e
BCC: 3sftm@MrBig.net.www.e
BCC: 11sftm@MrBig.net.www.e
Subject: Lab 2
Time: Dec 8, 09:12

A trained fur ball is hardly going to strike fear into the hearts off my enemies. Still, I suppose it show's promise. Much as I hate two, I will wait to sea how those dreadbeast embryos go. Though the minuet that Miss la de da fails me is the minuet I take her in for torturing. She's not fishing out WWWOS agents like I'd hoped. Not at all.

Your Boss and Overlord
Mr Big

## •16•

# THE APPETIZER

"PRRRT." QUETZEE BUTTED HIS head against Lilly's. "Prrrtssz."

She opened her eyes. "Go away, Quetzee. Let me sleep just a few more minutes."

Forked tongue flicking in and out, Quetzee licked Lilly's cheek. "Prrrt." Daintily, he leapt down from the bed, jumped up onto the dresser, and bashed the light switch a couple of times.

"No food left," Lilly said, as if he might understand.

He didn't. Reaching out his paw he swatted the switch another couple of times for luck.

Lilly took the hint and dragged herself out of bed.

"Ssss," Quetzee ducked under her feet.

She barely avoided falling on him. "Watch out!"

He backed off into the corner, hissing louder. Not ideal, but at least she had the chance to get dressed.

A moment later he looked up at her. "Prrrt?" He was such a forgiving wee soul.

"Come on, you," she said and opened the door.

Tail up, he headed over. "Prrrt." He brushed against her legs, looking up at her adoringly.

Lilly sighed and picked him up before rushing out. No exploring today, she had a hungry wee critter to feed.

From the safety of her shoulder, Quetzee bared his teeth to everyone passing by. Then he reached out a paw to a minion who passed too close.

The minion dodged. "Control your beastie," she muttered, scowling from a safe distance.

Lilly ducked around the corner, and hurried to the lab. It would be just her luck if Quetzee decided to eat one of the guards on the way – he certainly looked hungry enough.

Opening the door, Lilly was greeted by an odd gulping sound, as if one of the animals was choking.

"Missy!" Heart racing, Lilly fumbled for the light switch.

Quetzee jumped up onto the lab bench, and bashed the switch on and off like a strobe light – spotlighting a lumpy figure on the gurney, chest heaving dramatically.

"Missy!" Lilly called again, rushing over to see if there was anything she could do for the girl. But it wasn't Missy at all, it was Brian. A camera hovered over him, attracted by the noise of – not exactly choking – but snoring. Each rasping intake of breath punctuated by a nasty choking sound, and an exhale like a chainsaw.

Where was Missy?

There was something else. Another noise. Lilly turned around. Definitely not Quetzee. Tired of swatting the light switch, he was slinking toward the gurney, rump quivering.

Lilly peered underneath. "Missy?" And there she was, awake at last, sobbing quietly, her arms wrapped tightly around her legs.

"You're alright. You're alright, everything's fine," Lilly said trying to coax Missy out of her hiding place.

"Prrrtssz." Quetzee said. He rushed at them and skidded, complaining in a loud screeching wail as he careened into the girls.

Missy squealed and huddled further under the bed.

Quetzee shook himself and skittered up Lilly's shoulder.

"Good Quetzee," Lilly said absently stroking the critter as he chittered from his vantage. "You're safe, you know," she told Missy. "He won't bite. You can come out now."

Missy didn't move, just stared at Quetzee and Lilly, her eyes wide with fright.

"Look at me." Lilly caught Missy's jaw in her hand. "Look at me," she repeated firmly. "Stop squealing. We'll be fine. I'll help you. Quetzee will help both of us. You understand? The bite was just an accident."

Missy nodded, tears pouring down her cheeks. "I know. Accident," she said between sobs, before finally catching her breath and composing herself.

"Good," Lilly said. "Gotta keep a brave face now, don't we?" She risked a wink, hoping the camera wouldn't take it for anything nefarious. "Now, what should we do next? I'm game for cleaning out the lion enclosure. As I've told you before, there's no excuse for neglecting innocent critters."

"What about almost dying?" Brian asked with a yawn so large the camera in front of him would've had an excellent view of his tonsils. "Anyway, Missy's been through enough. Why don't you leave her be."

"I was only joking," Lilly said. "Well, mostly. Because Squidge pulled off a small miracle last night, now we don't have to worry so much about the dreadbeasts. So I thought today would be the perfect day to get this place in order. Missy could clean out a couple of smaller cages, while you and I sort out the lions."

"You can't be serious." Brian swung his legs over the gurney.

"I'm perfectly serious. It needs doing. Besides, everyone knows the cure for crying is hard work."

"What? Working cures crying?" Brian said. "Who told you that?"

"My parents. They also told me it's the best cure for almost dying. So I guess it's two for one. Missy should get scrubbing – for her own good."

Missy shook her head so her untidy hair fell over her face. "Your parents lied. And they don't sound very nice either."

The lab was silent except for the soft rustle of animals, as Lilly tried not to think too hard about what Missy had said.

"Sorry," Missy said, almost too soft to hear. Not to Lilly, but to Brian. Very weird.

Brian swallowed and rubbed his face. "It's okay," he said. "Anyway Lilly, why don't you let me do the smaller animals for Missy?"

"No, we're cleaning out the lion cage," Lilly said. "Just as soon as I've fed Quetzee."

"That monster should be in a cage," Brian muttered. "It's far more dangerous than the lions."

"*You* should be in a cage," Lilly retorted, and hurried off to organise Quetzee's bottle.

When she got back, Missy was still sulking under the bed. "If you like, you could feed Quetzee," Lilly offered, feeling sorry for the girl. She looked wretched.

Missy shook her head. Tears dripping from her red-rimmed eyes.

"How about organising breakfast? You know it would be a big help. And it *might* cure your crying problem."

Missy cried harder, and Brian glared at Lilly. But then he often glared at her for no reason at all. This time was worse though, because she was trying to help.

At least he offered to fetch breakfast.

When he returned, Missy said she wasn't hungry, and then refused to grab a rag when Quetzee burped a little milk over the floor. "It's your creature, you clean up its sick."

Squidge arrived all blotchy and panda-eyed, insisting he had to focus on his DNA work. "There are just a few things I want to check before we decide which embryo to place in the AW."

"Fine." Lilly gritted her teeth. "Brian, you're cleaning cages with me."

Brian hesitated.

"Now. Before we go the same way as Squidge's Prof."

Brian followed her into the menagerie reluctantly. At least he was following orders.

As they entered, Quetzee jumped down from her shoulders. The animals, especially some of the larger mammals, snarled and roared as he prowled around their cages.

Brian watched Quetzee suspiciously. "Are you sure you should leave him loose like that?"

"He'll be fine, come on." Lilly took a large squeegee mop, opened the cage's safety-catch, and walked in.

Brian, always nervous around the larger creatures, grabbed an electric goad as well as a squeegee. Gingerly, he sidled through the cage door, and began to help push lion dung into the drain. Not that he spent much time doing that. Mostly he watched the lions.

Lilly kept an eye on them too, keeping them at bay with her squeegee when she needed to. That, and shovelling dung about, really raised a sweat.

They were almost finished when Squidge pushed open the menagerie door, and Quetzee rushed out.

"Masticating mites!" Lilly rushed out of the lion cage, slamming the cage door shut behind her. "Putrefying pestilence! Squidge, you've let him out."

"What?" Squidge, still holding the door open, looked behind him. "Who?"

Not stopping to explain, Lilly dropped her squeegee "Quetzee! Quetzee!"

"Um, what about me?" Brian yelled from inside the cage.

"You'll be fine." Lilly pushed past Squidge, who was standing in the doorway like a statue. Worried Dr Deathless or one of his flunkies might steal him, she chased her precious creation down the corridor. "Quetzee! Here, boy!"

"Prrrtssz," Quetzee replied, from not so far away. He looked suggestively toward the kitchens.

"Come on, Quetzee. Come back." Lilly crept forward and tried to grab him.

He dodged Lilly, and scampered back into the menagerie.

Lilly raced in after him, closing the door of the lab just as Brian started screaming, "No-argh! He-elp!"

"Feline faeces!" Lilly swore as the lioness dragged Brian by the arm into the corner of the cage. His goad dropping uselessly onto the blood-stained concrete.

§

To: MrBig@MrBig.net.www.e
From: Security@MrBig.net.www.e
Time: Dec 24, 09:11
Subject: Lab 2 Menagerie

Looks like we really are going to need another minion this time.

§

To: Security@MrBig.net.www.e
From: MrBig@MrBig.net.www.e
Subject: Lab 2 Menagerie
Time: Dec 24, 09:17

Don't worry, I've got plenty of job applicants on hand after that Melissa disaster.

Your Boss and Overlord
Mr Big

•17•

# HELP

**BRIAN SCREAMED AS THE** sound of crunching bone – his crunching bone – echoed around the menagerie.

"Panthera's peritoneum[16]," Lilly rushed to the cage. She heaved the cage door up, grabbed her squeegee, and let the cage door clang behind her. "What did you think you were doing?" she demanded, but only got grunts and shrieks of pain for an answer.

The lion, its teeth still buried deep in Brian's arm, shook him from side to side.

"Back!" Lilly commanded, waving her squeegee.

The two lions stared at her, unflinching, and with deadly keen interest.

Lilly swallowed. On second thoughts, racing into a cage with two overexcited lions, armed with nothing more than a squeegee, might not have been the smartest move. Determined not to be eaten, she tried not to think about what Quetzee might be up to, and jabbed the sponge end at the lions.

The lions slowly retreated a short distance, the lioness

16 The peritoneum is the membrane lining the cavity of the abdomen and covering the abdominal organs. If it belongs to a Panthera (the genus of big cats that includes lions, tigers and panthers), it's something you'll want to stay well away from. *VF*

stolidly growling through a mouthful of Brian's arm. Her big golden eyes never quite turning away, she watched Lilly intently. Too clever, that one.

"I think you forgot something," Squidge said helpfully from a safe distance outside the cage. He was pointing at something near her feet.

"What? – oh." Brian's electric goad was just to her right. Sidestepping, she poked it with her foot, flipping it into the air …

The lion shuffled excitedly, hindquarters lowering as if to pounce.

… Lilly grabbed at the tumbling stick, and fumbled. It clattered on the concrete, and bounced up …

The lion, growling louder than ever, leapt.

... Swallowing her fear, Lilly caught the goad two-handed, and thrust it at the lion's jaw.

*Bzzzz.*

Yelping horribly, the lion twisted away leaving a clear path for Lilly to rescue Brian. And yet she hesitated – the lion's yelps of pain echoing in her ears.

Brian, almost unconscious on the floor, moaned. His life in her hands, Lilly swallowed and gripped the goad tighter. She thrust it at the lioness, flinching at the squeal-growl of pain as the lioness let Brian's arm fall from her jaws.

Turning her attention from Brian, the lioness snapped angrily at the goad. Her paw shot out, sharp claws raking through the front of Lilly's lab coat.

"That was my best lab coat," Lilly objected, stumbling backward. Blood seeped through the gash and pain flared in her abdomen. She righted herself as the lioness swiped at her again, hit the goad with her paw, yelped, and veered away.

Seeing Lilly was vulnerable, the lion shook his moth-eaten mane, roared fearsomely, and approached. His lips snarled up around his blackened teeth, breath hot, rot-sweet, and sulphurous.

Dangerous. But not as dangerous as the lioness. Her intelligent eyes sized Lilly up, then she licked her bloody maw and turned back to Brian. His blood was everywhere.

"Squidge, help!" Lilly yelled. There was no way she could rescue Brian and keep two over-excited lions at bay.

"I do not see why I should risk my life for him," Squidge said. "He is a minion. You know Mr Big has plenty of those."

"Squidge, you idiot. We're *all* minions! And I'm the minion in charge, remember? So, do as I say."

Squidge shrugged. "You are the boss, boss. But if you ask me—"

"I didn't *ask* you," Lilly said, trying not to panic. "Now hurry." The lioness was circling around the edge of the cage, just out of Lilly's reach. If Lilly wasn't careful, the beast would get between her and the exit, but there was nothing she could do to cut the lioness off, not without exposing Brian.

"Squidge! Now!"

Squidge rolled his eyes, but did as he was told and rushed in, holding nothing more than a retort stand[17] clasping a feeder bottle.

He was brave, she'd give him that. And because of that, the lions retreated. Or maybe it was because Quetzee had rushed inside too, and was darting to and fro under Squidge's feet in excitement.

"Here, take this." Lilly shoved Brian's goad at Squidge.

He waved the goad back and forth, protecting her right flank.

The lions watched, as if mesmerised by the electrified stick.

Screwing up her courage, Lilly grabbed the barely conscious Brian, trying not to look too closely at his arm hanging limply in a shattered bloody mess. She wanted to run. Instead,

---

17 A retort stand is used to hold test tubes and other glassware. It has a clamp that can be moved up and down. *VF*

she backed up, keeping the cage bars to her left.

To her right, Squidge matched her progress. Quetzee circled them both protectively as they inched toward the cage door one half-step at a time.

Padded feet haunted Lilly like a waking nightmare, as the lions began to follow. The lion stopped only to snuffle his maw into a patch of blood Brian had left behind. Then he looked up and bounded forward with renewed interest.

"Shoo!" she yelled.

The lion wheeled sideways – a little.

Don't relax yet, Lilly told herself as she and Squidge reached the exit, the lions hovering just out of reach of Squidge's flailing goad.

Squidge turned to open the door and the lions surged forward.

Grabbing the goad from Squidge, Lilly caught the in-rushing lion on the nose.

It wheeled back with barely a squeal, and Brian, little more than a dead weight in her arms, slipped.

"Vegetative ventricles[18]," she cursed, struggling to regain her grip on Brian and defend against two lions at the same time.

The door groaned. Hours seemed to pass as it creaked open.

The lions watched on, whiskers twitching, as Squidge exited into a flock of swirling cameras. He'd left her in the cage alone with a semi-conscious Brian, and two lions.

Lilly held Brian tight, threw her goad at the lioness, and turned and ran out the cage door. Claws raked the tail of her lab coat as she passed through. Not that it mattered, the thing was totally ruined.

Squidge slammed the door shut behind them. "Gosh,

---

18 Ventricle is a hollow part of cavity in any organ, but is usually associated with the heart or brain. *LL*

Brian's arm is a mess," he said.

Brian mumbled, looked down at the shattered ulna stabbing out of his almost completely severed arm, and fainted again.

His dead-weight too much for Lilly, they both collapsed to the ground.

The lions roared and surged against the door of the cage.

Quetzee hissed back at them, and they flinched momentarily before surging forward again with a deafening roar. Was the door starting to buckle?

"Simian smeg—[19]!" Lilly rolled from under Brian's dead weight, and grabbed a goad from the wall. It hit the lion's shoulder with a long angry *bzzzz*. The lion squealed, a higher pitch this time, and reared backward.

"Draconian dung," Lilly swore again, over the roaring of angry lions.

And who could blame them? She'd stolen their legitimate kill. And they'd been hurt. Hopefully only a sore paw and injured pride, but today had been a real step backward in her plan to put a stop to the neglect and mistreatment of the animals in her care. Guiltily, Lilly turned away from the lioness' accusing eyes, part of her just happy to be safe for the moment.

The flock of hovering cameras jiggled excitedly, calming only when the lioness stopped roaring and licked at her paw.

Where was Brian? She'd left him not two feet away on the floor. Was he obscured by the small flock of cameras? No, he was gone, and replaced by – Pinhead?

What was Pinhead doing here?

Lilly rushed over in alarm.

Pinhead was lifting Brian onto the trolley, with little help from Squidge, who was babbling, "I have gloves. Do you

19 Simians are a group of primates including monkeys apes and humans. Smeg is a brand of appliance, but Lilly insists she said no such thing. *VF*

want gloves? It would be safer."

Together Lilly and Pinhead wheeled Brian into the lab, while Quetzee weaved back and forth through the legs of the gurney, occasionally stopping to lap at Brian's blood.

Missy was still whimpering under her gurney as Lilly held the swinging door open for Brian's trolley.

"Missy, some help here!" Lilly ordered.

"Who cares?" Melissa moaned, without bothering to look up. "We're all going to die anyway."

"I care." Lilly said. "So get the first aid kit, or Brian will die right now!"

"Brian?" Melissa blinked. "Holy cow, what happened?" She ran and grabbed the kit, while Lilly tied a tourniquet. Squidge wandered off shouting something that sounded remarkably like, "Eureka."

Quickly, Lilly pulled out everything she thought she might need. "Needle, thread, bandage, surgical saw? That'll do." A hospital would be better. Unfortunately, she was Brian's best hope. And even if she wasn't a surgeon, at least she'd had some experience operating on animals.

"Anaesthetic?" she asked Missy.

The girl promptly handed her a vial marked, *single dose, operation strength for minions.*

Lilly injected Brian with it, before carefully checking his arm. It was a mess of torn flesh, veins and arteries, not to mention the nerves. The damage was extensive from the shoulder down, but the forearm was thoroughly mangled. There was no way she could get it functional again. Biting her lip, she weighed his options. It did not take long. With her lack of experience, Brian's best hope of survival was to simply remove his arm from the elbow.

Taking a breath she lifted the hacksaw. And put it down. Melissa was hovering over her shoulder, clutching the first aid kit. Pinhead also looked on. His expression unreadable.

*No pressure,* Lilly lied to herself.

Finding a marker, she carefully drew a line just above his elbow. Satisfied it was straight, she started to make the first tentative cut.

Blinking awake, Brian took one look at that hacksaw and screamed in a pitch more piercing than an electrocuted lion. He tried to hit Lilly with his good arm. "Sod off, that's my arm."

"Perhaps I should have let the lion feed on you," Lilly growled. "It'd be a less agonising death than gangrene."

Brian moaned, his face contorted in pain.

Lilly thumped her head, clearly the anaesthetic wasn't working. The stress of the last few days was beginning to show, or maybe it was just the stress of the moment, either way she'd been unbelievably stupid. "Missy! What anaesthetic did you give me?" She waved the hacksaw for emphasis.

"Acet ... Atelyl ... " Missy held up the vial.

"Acetylsalicylic acid? Aspirin? Operation strength indeed. We got anything else? Where's the stuff I used for Brian?" While she waited for Missy to rummage through the kit, Lilly wiped the blade clean and re-sterilised it.

Brian screamed. This time he tried to scramble off the gurney, but Missy handed over a needle of *Important minion 70-90kg, operation strength Papaver somniferum*[20], and Lilly sank it into him.

Brian sighed, and collapsed back onto the gurney.

"Poor Brian," Missy said, turning to Lilly. "How could you let this happen?" She didn't wait for an answer. "You know it's your fault. He should never have been cleaning that cage. Not with the lions in it. Even *I* know that."

Lilly frowned. Was it her fault? Probably. She hadn't given

20 A dangerous narcotic that hospitals can use for pain relief. *VF*

nearly enough thought to safety procedures. But now wasn't the time, she shook the doubts from her head, and clipped the heart-rate monitor onto Brian's finger.

*Ping. Ping. Ping.*

Missy watched the readout avidly. (Probably to avoid looking at the arm she was helping to hold.)

"Squidge, you wouldn't want to help over here?" Lilly shouted.

"Bit busy, I have all the important dreadbeast calculations to do," Squidge shouted back without even turning around. "I am sure you are doing fine."

Gritting her teeth, Lilly got back to work. She was most of the way through sawing off the arm when Squidge came over waving a fist-full of papers. "This is so … What *are* you doing?"

"What does it look like? I'm sawing off Brian's arm."

"I told her not to," Brian murmured, a happy smile on his face, a trace of drool running down his chin.

"I guess that is good. And never mind, Brian," Squidge said cheerfully. "We can attach an orangutan arm for you. It will be almost as good as new. And great for climbing trees."

"Thah's nice," Brian murmured.

"What! Don't be ridiculous," Lilly said. "You want me to hack an arm off a poor innocent orangutan?"

"Don't you think Brian is more important than an animal?" Missy demanded.

"What!? No, it's completely unfair to expect an orangutan to lose his arm, because we were careless. Brian will just have to learn from this mistake and move on."

Squidge stared at Lilly. "I suppose I could clean up Brian's arm and reattach it," he said thoughtfully. "It will take a while."

"What!" Lilly yelled. "You could have mentioned this

earlier. Like when I was asking for help?"

"It *is* a terrible waste of my time," Squidge said, either by way of explanation, or complaint. Lilly wasn't exactly sure, but she sure was angry. And so was Missy. "Squidge!" both girls yelled at the same time.

He seemed to get the hint. "I'll scrub up then," he said.

"You do that." Lilly turned back to see Missy put her hand to her mouth in horror – as the heart-rate monitor's *ping* stuttered.

"Lilly!" Missy yelled as Brian shuddered, and stopped breathing.

§

To: Security@MrBig.net.www.e
From: MrBig@MrBig.net.www.e
Subject: Lab 2 Menagerie
Time: Dec 24, 09:32

Surprisingly my live feed shows the minion's not quite dead yet. Although maybe—

# •18•

# PAUL THE POISONER

MISSY STOOD THERE, HAND to her mouth, staring at Brian.

"Oxygen kit," Lilly yelled. "Now!"

The girl started to move – and froze again, pointing. Something was hunched over the dark pool of Brian's blood.

Quetzee – eagerly lapping at the blood.

"Yes, it's great Quetzee is eating," Lilly said over her shoulder. "But I need that oxygen kit, now!"

Missy clutched her stomach and made choking, heaving noises. Lilly didn't have time to wonder if this was some kind of delayed reaction to Quetzee's poison, or if she really was that squeamish. "CPR, now!" Lilly yelled, running over to grab the oxygen kit herself. "Squidge!"

The boy seemed to be going over to help Brian, but when she took the oxygen kit off its hook and looked back, Squidge had taken up the black marker pen, the one she had used on Brian's arm, and was writing complex calculations on the lab bench.

"Squidge!" she yelled. "Missy! Why in the Web aren't either of you performing CPR?" she demanded, rushing over to do it herself.

Missy's shocked eyes turned to Lilly. "I don't know how."

"Ugh! Disgusting!" Squidge said, completing an equation, and underlining the answer. "CPR spreads Hep B, Hep A, and Hep C, and who knows what else."

"What?" Missy said. "Brian doesn't really have any of those diseases, does he?"

"No," Lilly said. "Almost certainly not," she added. "And that's not the point. Brian … could have … died." Trying to keep track of chest compressions, and talk at the same time, wasn't exactly easy.

"Better him than me," Squidge muttered. Besides I need to finish these equations if you want me to operate."

"Squidge, you listen to me." Lilly was getting really angry. Next time it could be her on the gurney, and who would make sure they did their jobs then? "We are a team. We need to stick together, or the next time you're injured don't expect me to help."

"Fine." Squidge shrugged.

"Good." Lilly decided to take that as a *yes* and readjusted the oxygen.

Missy patted Brian's uninjured arm. "Brian stay with me," she said soothingly. "Stay with us. We need you."

"Much good that's likely to do," Lilly muttered under her breath, and started another round of compressions.

"He had better survive after all this," Squidge said. "We are so far behind, and you always seem to need extra hands to clean out the cages."

"Very funny," Melissa muttered. "Was your orangutan arm just a joke too?"

"Funny?" Squidge muttered. "Brian would be better off with an orangutan arm. Brachiation would enable him to swing between the cages. He would almost never need the crane."

"Focus, Squidge," Lilly said. "We need to save Brian."

"I am. I am wondering what could have happened to cause Brian to crash like that."

"Shock? Loss of blood?" Lilly examined Brian's inert body while once again taking a short break from compressions. He remained unresponsive. "Do we have a defibrillator[21] around here?"

"No. Too easy to rig as a weapon."

*Unlike the giant surgical saw and the equally giant scissors*, Lilly thought. But then again, this place was full of crazy people, who were more scared of Quetzee than of buffed goons with guns.

"Exsanguinated endocrinologists![22] Oxygen and compressions aren't working." Lilly began another series of compressions anyway. Now the idea was in her head it was hard not to think about a hundred different ways she could use a defibrillator as a weapon. She had to refocus on how to save Brian. "I don't ... get it ... it's like ... he just ... went into ... shock and ... stopped breathing – like anaphylactic[23] ... *putrefying plasma*[24]! I need adrenaline[25] now!"

Squidge was already opening the drawer on the word "anaphylactic." On the word "now", he filled a giant needle, plunged it into Brian's chest, then jumped back.

"Ugh." Missy looked away as Brian spasmed, coughed, and started choking – sick pooling down his front.

Lilly couldn't blame him, she could barely manage to keep her own sick in – and she didn't have an enormous needle

---

21 A defibrillator is a machine used to restart the heart. *VF*

22 Exsanguinated is a fatal amount of bloodloss (think vampire) and an endocrinologist is a doctor specialising in hormones. *VF*

23 An allergic reaction that can cause death. *VF*

24 Putrefying plasma would roughly translate as rotting blood. *VF*

25 Also known as epinephrine, this is the hormone most commonly associated with fight or flight, and is the medicine of choice for anaphylaxis *LL*

sticking out of her chest. "Um – don't you think that was excessive?" she asked Squidge.

"No," said Squidge. "Not if you wanted me to save him. That is what you wanted? I thought we were supposed to be making a new improved dreadbeast, but you said we needed to rescue Brian. To do so I will need a hazard kit and some universal plasma."

"Lilly, wondering exactly what Squidge might know about the lions that she didn't, turned to organise the blood when Dr Deathless appeared.

"Idiots. Fools. Incompetents," he raged. "Do I have to do everything myself? I'd replace the lot of you, but I don't have the time to train up another minion let alone a whole lab before the Spring Catalogue of Evil."

He threw a bag of haemo-pure at Squidge.

Squidge caught it automatically, the vivid red blood in the bag stark contrast to his ashen complexion, and the white hazard suit spooling around his ankles.

"d ... d ... dr ... Deathl—"

"Yes, we all know who I am."

Hands shaking, Squidge looked askance at Dr Deathless, before turning back to focus on his work. He hooked up the bag and plugged in the lure, once, twice – on the third time it went in properly.

Dr Deathless lounged against a bench, grinning at Squidge's discomfort. "You two have really taken the rhino by the horn – or should that be the lion by the tail?" He laughed. "Two helpers, and you've almost killed both of them. A hundred percent injury rate. My congratulations Esquire Grey. That's an even better record than I had testing gelignite traps on unsuspecting minions."

Squidge squealed in outrage. "Brian might be a nuisance, but I like him. And anyway I do not murder assistants."

Lilly glared at Dr Deathless. "Squidge, please ignore the overblown nobody. We're too busy to listen to the likes of him."

Dr Deathless' laugh sounded hollow, as if he'd forgotten what humour really meant. "The young Esquire can't help it. He probably injected himself with that squealing rat serum he made last year."

"Did not. Well, just the once. And it was an echolocation experiment." Squidge's mouth snapped shut as if he had said too much. His hands balled into little fists. "And … I … you just call me Squidge. All right?"

"I seem to remember Mr Big closed the experiment down because your rats were so noisy the boss could hear them from his rooms."

"Was not. Did not. And that experiment was classified. So just you shut up!"

Dr Deathless performed a mocking bow. "I'm going." He laughed so horribly Quetzee startled away from the blood he'd been lapping, and ran for the safety of Lilly's shoulder.

Missy, who'd remained quiet and unnoticed all this time, shrieked and shrank backward as Quetzee flitted past.

Also shaken, but for different reasons, Squidge sat down on the nearest lab stool. Hands trembling, he began putting on a hazard suit.

"There, there," Lilly said. "Everything's better, isn't it? Now, tell me, what did Brian get from the lions? Venom of some kind?"

"Venom of some kind," Squidge echoed as he finished doing up the hazard suit. "At least I think so. It was before my time. Paul the Poisoner, I believe." He snapped on gloves and started inspecting Brian's arm carefully, cleaning the flesh and cutting off anything too mangled. She had no idea how he was going to fix the crushed and splintered bone.

"You need anything else? Clamps? Some thread for stitching?" Lilly asked.

"Yes. If you go to the fridge, you will find my patented hormone and nutrient infused body-glue."

"Missy?" Lilly asked hopefully, rummaging in the drawer for clamps.

Missy didn't reply, not even when Lilly repeated the question and waved her hand in front of Missy's face. Nothing, not a flicker.

"Weasel's waste-products, what use are you?" Squidge muttered.

Lilly shook her head and went to get the glue – not looking forward to playing theatre nurse for the rest of the morning, but not wanting to miss a moment of the operation either. However horrible, this was an important learning opportunity that could help her save lives.

Still, in the minute it took to collect all the stuff, she realised there were a few important questions she needed to ask Squidge. And now, while he was in a hazard suit up to his elbows in blood, and he couldn't escape into a computer screen – was the perfect opportunity.

"So those sonic rats – you used bat DNA for the echo-location? Did you?"

"Grunt."

"Any chance I could see?—"

"Pass a clamp."

"What about those lions? You know what poison that Paul fellow used?"

"Ugh. Pass the scalpel."

And so on. By the end of the operation, Lilly was about to pass a scalpel with force. How dare he keep the results of important experiments from her? Was she not a part of the team – supposedly the leader? Not that she had any illusions about that. She was just where the buck stopped.

Fortunately though, the operation itself was going well. According to Squidge, his glue would not only adhere the bone and flesh, but also discourage bacteria and encourage re-growth of nerves, capillaries[26] and even arteries. If it was anyone else, she'd have been incredulous, but Squidge was some kind of unbalanced genius, so, she figured, it just might work.

Lilly looked about. Squidge wasn't around, but he never left the lab for long. *Best use the opportunity*, she thought, rushing over and typing his password: *ATGCMagshn* into his laptop. Sonic rats and poisoned lions were experiments that seemed worth chasing up. The lions in case they bit someone else, but the sonic rats were something Squidge definitely didn't want her to know about – which made them all the more interesting.

A noise behind Lilly's shoulder made her jump.

It was only Missy. "You want a cup of tea?" she asked.

"Oh, yes, thank you," Lilly said.

As soon as her heart stopped pounding she found a dreadbeast file and pretended to look at it. Thinking how unfortunate it was that Missy would suddenly decide to be helpful now. But at least there was colour coming back to her cheeks.

Missy hovered for a moment and wandered off. She seemed quiet, almost subdued, as she turned away.

Continuing her search through the old lab files Lilly failed to find any mention of lions. Or Paul the Poisoner. Still, one file caught her eye—

The Title *Experiment 97 – Echolocation* hovered above solid-black redacted lines. It seemed everything underneath had been thoroughly obliterated except a handwritten note

---

26 Capillaries: Tiny blood vessels. *VF*

including the gene – *Tg(uhf1-15)EsqG* and a few *ands* and *buts*. At least that gave her somewhere to start.

She searched for the gene, it was mentioned in folder titled *Supersonic*. Included were half a dozen papers and a heavily encrypted file helpfully labelled *97*. Lilly broke through a layer of encryption by using a file named *bug-breaker*, but the file still looked like a fuzzy picture. She searched his computer for more keys, and tried some common algorithms, but nothing worked.

Someone was breathing over her shoulder. She whipped her head around to see Missy again, back with two steaming mugs.

"Lilly exited the program, and turned to grab the tea. "Thanks. Good to see you've decided to turn over a new leaf."

"Yeah," Missy said. Her lack of enthusiasm evident. "I'm just following orders."

"Anyway, Lilly," Missy said. "I heard you took Quetzee to our room. I'm not—"

"Quetzee?" Lilly interrupted, suddenly noticing his absence. "Where is he? And thinking about it, where's Squidge? He should be here by now."

"Never mind Squidge. I was saying I'm not sleeping in the same room as that creature of yours."

"That's okay," Lilly said. "You can sleep in the lab if you'd rather. Now, please if you'd just help me look for Q—"

"No." Missy's jaw set.

"Missy!"

Missy shook her head. "I'm sorry. What I meant to say was I won't sleep in the lab, but I will help you look for Quetzee."

But there was no sign of him.

*Why hadn't she noticed earlier?* Frantic, Lilly rushed out into the corridor to the menagerie. She ran across the front of the aisles, but she couldn't see him. Squidge was there though, wrestling with a cage. "Squidge, there you are," Lilly said. "What are you doing with that cage? And have you seen – ?"

Lilly blinked in shock. Squidge wasn't wrestling with a cage, he was trying to drop it on top of Quetzee. Squidge almost succeeded, but Quetzee swerved out from under the falling cage, chittering angrily. He rushed to the door, up onto a bench, and started bashing at the light switch.

"You hungry?" Lilly asked, sending Squidge an evil look.

"Prrrtssz," Quetzee said and followed her into the storeroom. Minutes later they were back in the lab with Quetzee curled up in her lap sucking greedily from a bottle of milk. He looked so contented and peaceful – until he vomited over Lilly's lab coat.

Thinking he'd drunk the milk too fast, Lilly tried again. Slower. This time he promptly fell asleep. Five minutes later he woke up and vomited over her skirt.

"Emetic[27] Egrets, what am I going to do?!" Lilly said, not really asking, just angry, but Squidge replied anyway. "I'd keep him away from milk if I was you."

"Duh," Lilly said, rushing off for clean clothes and wondering what she was going to feed Quetzee on now, when Missy called out. "Brian's awake. He's all right. He's alright!"

"Great Christmas present this is," Brian said, pulling back his covers to reveal his heavily splinted arm.

"What?" Lilly said. "Christmas?"

"It is still December 24th?" Brian asked. "I didn't miss it, did I?"

"Wait … oh, oh yes, yes it is!" Squidge jumped about like a small kid. "It is Christmas tomorrow, how could I have forgotten? Only five hours and forty-four minutes to go."

---

27 Emetic: a substance causing vomiting. (Sorry if you didn't need to know that.) *VF*

"Asphyxiating[28] arachnids! It's Christmas Eve?! You mean the deadline is tomorrow? How are we ever going to be ready in time?"

"Do not worry, Miss," Squidge said. "The embryo is on track, so if we tidy up a bit now, tomorrow we can have the day off for Christmas. Maybe we will get some new lab equipment to play with."

"But it's Christmas Eve," Lilly said. "And we're working. I should be shopping. No, forget that, I want to go to bed for a week and have a personal shopper do all my Christmas shopping. Then go shopping for myself, anyway."

"Come on, Miss Lionheart," Squidge said, taking a step toward her. "Shopping? Really? Who would want to wander around buying things? Bore-ring."

Quetzee, having long since given up on the light switch, sauntered between them.

Squidge jumped and backed away. So did Missy, but Quetzee ignored her, and focused on bailing Squidge into a corner. Snarling, Quetzee darted in – and didn't bite. It soon became obvious he was avoiding biting the boy. Maybe Quetzee figured biting Squidge hadn't worked the first time, or maybe he'd tasted bad. Whatever the reason, Squidge soon figured it out and walked away.

With Quetzee hissing and spitting after him, Squidge called back to Lilly, "Maybe if you would be so kind, you could get me the blood sample from your critter and save me the time."

Intending to do no such thing, Lilly busied herself by tidying the lab for tomorrow's day off, shoving glassware into the sterilizer, and organising her notes.

Meanwhile Quetzee ran around the lab poking his head

---

28 Asphyxiating: lack of air to breathe. But how this pertains to arachnids at Christmas is anybody's guess. *VF*

through bars, butting his head up against Plastech cages, and hissing and carrying on. It was upsetting so many of the critters, the lab was in an uproar.

Exasperated, Lilly called him over and fed him a big fat rat – the one that had bit Squidge on her first day. Then she did her final rounds, checking all the animals, with Quetzee riding high on her shoulders. He chattered happily, as if he thought he owned the place. Afterward, Lilly strolled around the facility, too pent up to eat, or sleep, while Quetzee accosted every idiot that patrolled the corridors with his chatter, as if he thought he owned them too.

As she walked the corridors, she thought about the fuzzy picture she'd seen earlier in the day. And the more she walked, the more she thought that it was a map of the bunker. Which meant she knew exactly how to get out once she'd passed the electric plate. And tomorrow night would be the perfect time to escape.

When Lilly opened the door to her room, Missy's bed was neatly made, and all her possessions were gone. She wondered where Missy was, but only for a moment. Happy to finally have a room to herself.

"Well done, Quetzee," Lilly said absently patting him on his fat stomach.

Quetzee liked the pat well enough, bobbing his head toward her for more. "Prrrtssz" he said enjoying the attention, before turning off the lights and curling up at the bottom of her bed.

§

*Dear Diary,*

*We saved Brian's life and his arm – and so much for the thanks we get. A few tears, some heartfelt thanks?*

*No. Not from anyone, least of all Brian. Or Missy. She's*

*always fawning over him, but when he really needed her help, where was she? Bet he thanked her.*

*It hardly seems fair. This has been the worst Christmas Eve ever – if you don't count the year poor little Freddie, my ultra-sweet bobcat-wolf cross, was put down, and just for mauling the kids next door. It wasn't like they didn't deserve it.*

*Still, Quetzee is getting really good at turning my lights off at night, proving he can be trained, and it stops me from having to get out of bed at least.*

§

To: MrBig@MrBig.net.www.e
From: Security@MrBig.net.www.e
Subject: LH
Time: Dec 24, 21:34

She's found the rat maps.

11sftm

§

To: Security@MrBig.net.www.e
From: MrBig@MrBig.net.www.e
Subject: It's on.
Time: Dec 24, 21:36

Meet me at midnight. You know where.

Your Boss and Overlord
Mr Big

§

•19•

# CHRISTMAS IN AN EVIL CRIMINAL MASTERMIND'S BUNKER

LILLY WOKE UP THINKING Christmas in this dump was like putting a Rottweiler into a sugar-plum fairy outfit – only to go to breakfast and find Mr Big had done exactly that. Poor Annie sat at the front of the mess-hall, scratched at her pink tutu and whined, until Mr Big thoughtfully distracted her with an oversized femur – still wearing a sock.

Meaning to disappear as quietly as possible, so she could make the most of her day off, Lilly popped a sleepy Quetzee onto her shoulder, grabbed a plate and started loading it with some tempting treats for them both.

Unable to wait, Quetzee jumped down, hooked a piece of greasy bacon with his claws, and scampered back up her arm. Fortunately nobody seemed to notice.

All she wanted was to escape to her room for a few hours alone time.

Just as she was trying to make a quiet exit, Squidge ran up to her, bouncing up and down like a particle that's just experienced fission – or like any other twelve-year-old boy hyped up on sugar on Christmas morning. "Miss, Miss! When do you think Santa is going to arrive?"

"Santa?" Lilly asked. "Um. How do you think Santa is

going to get into this bunker? There aren't exactly a lot of chimneys around."

"A chimney? What have chimney's got to do with Santa?" Squidge asked confused. "You do know Santa's just a man in a red suit?"

"Yes, Squidge," Lilly said, wondering if it was worthwhile trying to explain to him the difference between adult condescension and adult stupidity.

"I am so excited," he burbled. "Last year Santa gave me my very own DNA sequencer, several incubators, oh, and my very own lab."

"Really? How generous," Lilly replied, absently cutting Quetzee more slices of blue-mermaid tattooed *bacon*.

"Imagine Mr Big employing a genius and setting them up with everything they need to make the mutant creatures he wants."

"Yes, it was lucky Mr Big rescued me and brought me here after my mum and dad died in that very suspicious laboratory fire."

"Very *lucky*," Lilly muttered.

"Yes," Squidge said without a trace of irony, and raced off because he'd seen a thug in a Santa suit squeezing into the room.

"Ho, ho, ho. Merry Christmas," Pinhead shouted from under a skewed white beard. He scratched at it, and glared around the room. "Come and get your presents."

It sounded like a threat.

Determined to get out of there without raising any more attention – Lilly balanced the plate of treats in one hand, a cup of lousy coffee in the other, and rushed past Mr Big to the door. "Just checking up on your dreadbeast," she mumbled by way of an excuse as she passed by.

Mr Big's voice came booming after her. "A moment, Miss

Lionheart. I'm sure that the dreadbeast can live one more minute without you. After all, Santa has come all this way."

"Yes, sir," she said, forcing herself to breathe in and out slowly – in the way commonly believed to relieve stress – but in Lilly's experience never seemed to work.

Breathe in. Breathe out. A few more minutes of annoyance was a small price to pay for a whole day of peace.

"Hey Santa," Mr Big shouted at Pinhead. "What do you have for all of us today?"

Before Pinhead could answer, Missy came charging into the dining hall yelling, "Miss! Miss Lionheart! The dreadbeast – it isn't going ping properly."

"It seems that our Miss Lionheart is right," Dr Deathless said to the silent room.

Missy turned bright red and backed out the door, as Dr Deathless continued. "Apparently her dreadbeast couldn't live one more moment without her attention after all."

"What!? Seriously?" Squidge dashed out the door faster than a speeding photon.

"Arachnid Anuses," Lilly swore, trying to ignore the mean laughter behind her as she raced after Squidge, chased in turn by nearly a dozen thugs, Annie, and the boss himself.

As soon as they got to the lab, Squidge rushed over to the AW. Lilly pushed past and peered through the Plastech walls.

It was obvious at first glance that the embryo wasn't about to make it. And it was also obvious that some idiot had taken it out and tried to revive it – but that wasn't exactly something Lilly wanted the boss to know, lest he jump to some potentially fatal conclusions.

"Right. What's happening here?" Mr Big yelled at Missy. "Has somebody knocked over this incubator?"

"Not me," Missy said with an unsurprising eagerness to avoid admitting to what might be referred to as a *terminal error.*

"Something must have happened," Squidge muttered looking at the spilt embryonic fluid on the bench. "What does the video – oof!" He looked across accusingly at Missy, but before he could say anything, Missy interrupted. "Maybe it was that Squirrel-snake thing."

Lilly didn't blame her, after all any *accident* with the Boss' dreaded dreadbeast was likely to be more universally fatal than she, or anyone else on their team, would like. Even so, she wasn't about to let Quetzee to take the blame. "Quetzee was with me," Lilly said, patting him reassuringly. She needed to think quickly if she wanted to divert attention from Quetzee, and any incriminating video footage of whatever Missy might have done wrong.

"Um. Here we are." She turned off the incubator's alarm. Everything's fine." I'll just use these electrodes to tweak the nutrient level, and the embryo will be right as rain."

Squidge opened his mouth. Lilly glared at him and he shut it again.

She fumbled in the drawer for a battery and flicked a small electrical charge into the solution. The creature spasmed, not with life of course, but with electricity. "There we go." She smiled with false confidence – and hoped Mr Big knew so little science he wouldn't know electrodes don't actually do that much for nutrient levels. She even wondered if she could have incanted a magic spell, and Mr Big wouldn't have known any better.

Inconveniently, he knew a little more than Lilly thought.

"Shouldn't that machine be going ping?" he asked, pointing to the monitor. Lilly held in a sigh, and kept the smile plastered on her face.

Squidge opened his mouth. A worrying sign at the best of times, but especially troubling with the boss around – the whole concept of lying was something he seemed to struggle with. "Ah. No—"

Lilly elbowed him.

"Ow." Squidge looked at her, and then at Mr Big, and something must have clicked. "Um, er. Yes, absolutely. One minute," he said, and fiddled with the machine's wires under the boss' very watchful eye.

That minute stretched out like a year. Lilly hoped Mr Big would leave, but he just stood there, unblinking. "Hurry up," he growled. "I haven't got all day."

With a shake of his head, Squidge turned the machine back on.

Lilly cringed. Her throat tightened and her stomach clenched, as time stretched out – seemingly forever

Worst of all, in the moment she knew they were all about to be exposed as liars, Annie licked her lips in anticipation.

•20•

# A MOST UNEXPECTED AND UNWELCOME CHRISTMAS PRESENT

ANNIE'S TAIL WAS A blur. Her ears perked as she strained at her leash, as if she could smell the scent of dead dreadbeast clear as roses in summer.

Lilly smiled, mostly to hide a sudden urge to vomit. "I'm sure everything is fine," she fibbed. "The screen can be a bit slow to warm up, is all."

The boss' trigger finger twitched. And still, unsurprisingly, the monitor refused to display a heartbeat of any kind. Not a blip. Not a ping …

Squidge banged the table.

*Ping.* No. Couldn't be. *Ping … ping.* Impossibly, a steady heartbeat scrolled across the screen.

Missy clapped her hands in delight.

Had Squidge performed some kind of miracle and brought the embryo back to life? No, the sensors were pressed to Squidge's finger.

A rather obvious way to fake a heartbeat. Lilly tried not to look too disappointed.

Fortunately, Mr Big didn't notice, he was too busy jabbing his own pudgy finger at Lilly.

Quetzee hissed a warning, and backed off, but only a

carefully measured foot. "Your team fails to deliver for my Spring Catalogue of Evil, Miss Lionheart, and you'll be paying ultimate price, understand?" He stormed out, dragging Annie yelping piteously behind him.

Once Annie's yaps had faded, Missy turned to the screen and then back to Squidge. "If he finds out, our lives are worth two week old chewing gum."

"You panic too much," Squidge said. "Besides, we always knew this one was a throwaway. Remember? I have been working on improved versions."

"He'd better not find out about that either." Lilly glared at Missy. "Or I'm not the only one paying his *ultimate price*, understand?"

The girl's eyes widened and she nodded.

"Good." Lilly thought about sending Missy off to clean the simian cages as punishment. But that seemed mean. Just because Lilly's Christmas was ruined, she needn't spoil everyone else's. "Go on then, enjoy your day off. Squidge and I are going to be busy here for a while longer."

Missy flounced away, muttering.

"You could stay and clean cages if you like," Lilly said, offended that Missy should be so unappreciative of her generosity. But Missy had gone.

When the lab was quiet, Quetzee stretched – flicking his tail in Lilly's mouth before jumping to the ground. He zigzagged toward Squidge, feet skittering across the floor. Tongue flicking in and out, he raised his paws, and looked up with adoring eyes.

His head bowed over the artificial womb's computer readout, Squidge didn't seem to notice.

"Here you go, Quetzee," Lilly said trying to gain Quetzee's attention with a slice of bacon. He turned up his nose. Head cocked in fascination as Squidge removed the dead dreadbeast embryo, and pinned it out on a dissecting mat.

"Quetzee," Lilly called one last time, but the little minx darted under the bench, tail in the air. "You know, I don't have the time for games," she told him. "I need to concentrate. The next dreadbeast needs to be ready for the swanky Spring Catalogue of Evil. Whatever that is."

Quetzee, ignored her so she got to work going through the incubator readings, in case Squidge had missed something. Nothing seemed particularly out of place – a few too many excess free radicals, some odd proteins ... maybe heat related ... interesti—

A clatter-scrabble of paws on the bench-top alerted her something was wrong.

Squidge screamed.

Lilly turned just in time to see Quetzee jump down from the lab bench, the half-dissected embryo in his mouth.

"Snakes' bladders," Squidge cursed as Quetzee gulped down his very expensive breakfast. "I only looked away to grab a micro-retractor."

Lilly kicked the desk in frustration. "Now we'll never know what was wrong." Something Lilly instantly regretted as a camera floated into view. She threw some food at the wolverines to distract them.

"I think it was a temperature issue with the incubator," said Squidge. "I will fix it in a minute."

The minute turned into an hour, then two, as they both scoured through the latest design, *Dreadbeast Mark II.*

"You sure you don't want me to re-check the coding?" Lilly asked, totally frustrated. "I could go over the design specs for the hundredth time."

"No. I do not think that is a problem. Our specifications and coding are solid. I am confident version two will do well. It is just a shame the parts for the new AWs will take about a month to get here."

"Fantastic," she said.

"What?"

"Oh, not the broken AWs," Lilly said. "That's terrible. But I'd really appreciate this dreadbeast getting into the incubator ASAP, so I can get some sleep. I'm totally necrotic."

"Dead? You are not dead."

"It's an expression." Lilly frowned as she reset the AW. Cooler temperatures would slow growth. It was a gamble either way.

"You know it really is lucky it died," Squidge said. "You might have wanted me to keep the old version, the same way you decided to keep that Quetzee thing. And that would be terrible because *Dreadbeast Mark II* is so much better."

"Good," Lilly said, turning to go. "But this better be the last version."

"Wait," Squidge said. "You should take this." He handed Lilly a flower-shaped wire ornament. "Here, this is a remote alarm. If the AW detects any glitches, it will ring."

Reluctantly, Lilly pinned the contraption to her left shoulder.

"Dress nice for dinner," Squidge said as she ran out the door. "It is a fancy black tie event. Mr Big gets tetchy if people do not follow the dress code."

Lilly sighed. The black tie event would almost certainly turn into a black funeral event for anyone who didn't arrive properly dressed. Which was maybe for the best, given that she'd rather be dead than turn up at a function with clothes from Minions 'R' Us.

To avoid either fate, she raced off to find Brian – and therefore Missy. (With the luxury of not being kidnapped at gunpoint, Missy had a much better range of clothes. Clothes no longer be hanging conveniently in Lilly's bedroom, but if she asked nicely, she might be able to borrow a dress.)

It took Lilly half an hour to track down Missy, and another half hour to apologise. Mostly because she fluffed the first apology by saying, "I'm *sooo* sorry for saving your life, twice. And then letting you have the day off." Whereupon Missy pointed out her life wouldn't have needed saving if not for Quetzee. And today was a holiday anyway.

*Not for me*, Lilly thought, and bit her tongue. "I'm really sorry," she said through a false smile, trying to ignore Quetzee chittering from the safety of her shoulder. And trying even harder to ignore the fact that Missy's new room was nicer than hers – if a little further from the lab.

After much cajoling Missy lent her a green silk dress, and wriggled out of cleaning duty for two days.

Not entirely sure how she'd been outsmarted, but too tired to care, Lilly half-sleepwalked back to her quarters, and hopped into bed.

Quetzee curled up beside her.

Lilly closed her eyes gratefully—

There was a knock at the door.

"Go away."

Another knock.

"Go away! I'm just having a quick rest."

Knock … knock … Louder this time.

"I told you—"

Brian burst through the door. "We have to go, now! The boss has noticed."

"Oh, Troglodyte's testa![29]" Lilly said, jumping out of bed. *It was evening already?*

She grabbed up Missy's dress. "You go, I'll be right behind

29 Lilly was probably confused here, as a Troglodyte is a cave dweller, and a testa is the outer coat of a seed. Or maybe she was just complaining about her bad night's sleep as testa is also the Italian word for head

you."

Brian stepped outside as Lilly ditched her work clothes and pulled the green dress over her head. The bust gaped horribly, especially after she pinned on Squidge's AW monitoring *flower.*

The horror. Cursing, she stuffed a sock in each bra cup and raced after Brian.

As they stepped inside the Christmas festooned mess hall, Annie growled a welcome.

Lilly flinched, anticipating a Mr Big tantrum, but he gave them no more mind than a flicker of his eyebrows as they slipped into their seats.

Mr Big tapped his wine glass for silence. The room hushed immediately. "For what you are about to receive, you should be truly grateful – to me."

Everyone laughed dutifully and raised their mugs.

Pinhead Pat, Lilly's third most hated person in the world, stood up and raised his drink. "To Mr B—"

The sentence hung unfinished; not because Pat had forgotten the words, although he might have in the moment; and not because of any assassination attempt – but because an alarm rang and disrupted everything.

*Oh dear, this is bad*, Lilly thought, before a horrible realisation dawned. The noise was coming from the flower on her dress. Something was up with the new dreadbeast. And, more importantly, she was about to disrupt this very important event.

A gunshot reverberated, the bullet shrieking past her ear and blasting into the cook standing behind her. Hand to bleeding chest, he grunted as he fell onto an enormous platter of meat.

Quetzee rushed to see what was happening, but backed off as Annie bet him to it. Tongue flicking in and out, he began circling the dog.

"Quetzee!" Lilly hissed. It wouldn't look good if her pet killed Mr Big's.

"Quetzee!"

He looked disdainfully her way until Mr Big roared, *"Miss Lionheart!* Are you determined to ruin my Christmas?"

"No, Sir. No. Ow!" Lilly said as Quetzee jumped onto her shoulders. "It's just, er, unfortunately the dreadbeast is at a delicate stage. It's … " she struggled for words. Um – delicate." Which was true enough, and unfortunate enough, given that the dreadbeast had not only ruined her day off, it had killed a man, and was threatening to put a further crimp in her ability to breathe.

Dr Deathless smirked. "What're you waiting for? The Darwin Awards?"

"Boa bladders," Lilly muttered as she fled with Squidge close behind her.

Back in the dining hall, Mr Big could be heard loudly muttering something about Miss Lionheart not much needing her Christmas present, or her head – but it was only words and not actual gunshots, which Lilly appreciated. Even better, the boss didn't follow them this time.

"Why is this happening?" Lilly hissed to Squidge.

"I don't know," he replied, opening the lab door. "We rechecked everything … "

Ping … ping. Ping … ping. Ping … ping.

As Lilly looked around Quetzee jumped off her shoulder and began strutting toward the incubator, tail high.

Squidge shooed him back with a foot as he checked the machine with a quizzical expression. The monitor was definitely showing a steady beat.

"There's nothing even wrong, and your stupid alarm almost killed us," Lilly grumped.

"I will check it. You go without me."

But Lilly was too scared to go back to the dinner alone, so she found some cat treats and to tempt Quetzee with. He weaved in and out through her legs, baring his little fangs.

The alarm shrieked again.

Quetzee hissed and ran behind Esmeralda's cage.

"Hmm," Squidge said thoughtfully, adjusting the electronics past the lowest programmed limit.

After a moment the machine stopped squealing and Lilly breathed a sigh of relief. "Yup, definitely just the temperature. You think that's low enough?"

"I hope so. We cannot lower it further. Heat is critical to the amniotic sterilisation process." Squidge snapped on a pair of gloves and opened the lid.

Darting around the side of the cage, Quetzee sniffed, tongue flicking in and out.

In retrospect Lilly realised she should've been ready. As it was, she could only watch as Quetzee leapt onto the bench casually hooked his paw into the open incubator, and fished the embryo into his mouth. The small lump of quivering flesh hung from his teeth in a way that was unquestionably terminal.

"What?!" Squidge flailed at the fast retreating Quetzee.

"Quick, put another one in!" Lilly demanded.

Squidge shook his head. "We only have two embryos left. We cannot waste them."

"Squidge, shut up and put one in anyway. We have to get back to the dinner and pretend nothing is wrong before they send out a search party." She looked around. "Or one of those floating eyes turns up."

While Squidge popped another embryo in, Lilly put Quetzee into a Plastech cage – for his own protection. Paws up, he scrabbled and hissed, and almost broke her resolve with a heart-wrenching yowl. But, as she reminded herself, it was in his best interests to be safely out of Mr Big's way.

They slunk back into the dinner.

Mr Big glanced up, poker faced. "Lilliana Lionheart, Esquire Grey, so good of you to rejoin us."

Lilly smiled nervously as she made her way to where Brian and Missy were sitting – heads bent together in deep conversation.

"Anyway," Mr Big said, jumping up with an enormous grin that scared Lilly out of her wits. "Now that we're all here, I have an announcement to make.

"Esquire Grey, Miss Lionheart, seeing as you were… unavailable earlier, it's time to announce your Christmas present. So sit down, shut up, and don't make me shoot you by ruining my wonderful surprise again."

Dumbly, Lilly nodded, then shook her head, surveying his over-eager face with the dread a *Crocodile versus Minions* game show contestant must feel.

Mr Big smiled wider. "Now that the dreadbeast project is almost over, you'll want to take on something more challenging."

More challenging than the impossible?

"Something more exciting," he continued, oblivious that the Dreadbeast project was far from over.

Lilly, pale as a labcoat, found herself clutching onto Brian. (Much to Missy's annoyance, if her scowls were any indication.) Not sure that she could stand any more excitement, Lilly crossed her fingers and prayed it was a trip to a remote island.

"So, congratulations. Your present this year is three million pounds to spend on … " he opened Prof's book.

Lilly closed her eyes in dread, before reluctantly blinking them open – to see a busy page full of scales and flame and claws …

She could barely look. It couldn't be. But there it was in

vivid detail, charbroiled bodies scattered all around and licks of red-orange flame puffing out of its mouth – Prof's dragon.

Somehow she managed to squeeze a *thank you*, from between gritted teeth. Fortunately, nobody noticed her horror. Squidge was turning cartwheels and somersaults enough for the both of them. "We're going to make a dragon! We're going to make a fire breathing, flying dragon!

Shell-shocked, Lilly smiled and nodded on autopilot. Her desire to escape rekindled. *Can I afford to risk it? Can I afford not to risk it? Was that fuzzy image a map, or just hopeful thinking? And if it was a map, then why hadn't Squidge used it to escape? Only he had, hadn't he?*

A grating sound disturbed her thoughts. Enough for her to notice most people had finished their meals. And then she saw the source. The far wall was sliding open, revealing a fully enclosed cage Plastech cage the size of a boxing ring.

"Now, Ladies and Gentlethugs," Mr Big orated. "It is my pleasure to announce that tonight we have something special in our Monster Death Ring."

Veins and Basher stood forward.

"The Zombies … versus … "

Mr Big waved his arms for effect as a tarpaulin was whipped up on the opposite side of the cage. The crowd backed off with a gasp. What was it? Three red sensors tracked back and forth on top of a six-legged blackened-steel body. Attached to the body, a multitude of bladed weapons, waved in all directions.

Mr Big grinned. " … The Machine!"

# PART III - THRICE SHY

•21•

# MONSTER DEATH RING

**THE CAFETERIA WENT CRAZY.** Thugs and techs waved money in the air and pressed it into the hands of the bookies taking bets on Dr Deathless' zombies, or Dr Clarke's Machine.

Brian, cradling his injured arm to his chest, pushed forward to better see what was happening.

The only people hanging back were Missy, Squidge and Lilly as the six-legged machine scuttled toward the Monster Death Ring and stopped by the entrance – various knives, swords and spikes rotating and jabbing the air.

Was it remote controlled? Or did it control itself?

Mr Big's voice came over a loudspeaker prompting a resurgence of shouting, grabbing and pushing as last minute bets were exchanged. "All firearms have been confiscated, otherwise you will find the usual rules apply – there are no rules. And three, two, one … we are live!"

With all the fuss, Lilly felt she could safely duck out the door without being noticed. At the entrance she glanced back. Squidge and Missy were following her. Mr Big didn't seem to notice their departure. He was too focused on the adversaries as they stepped into the ring, the Plastech cage doors dropping into place behind them.

"Ugh." Missy shivered from the safety of the corridor. "I hope that horrible machine doesn't win. It gives me the creeps."

"And the zombies don't?" Lilly asked.

Missy shrugged. "I don't really think of them as zombies. They're not exactly scary like the ones in movies."

"They're scary enough," Lilly muttered.

How come you two aren't betting?" Squidge asked. "Everyone always bets. I would, but Dr Deathless is going to win, and I hate him."

"Darnation," said Missy. "Dr Deathless? Really? You should have said. Next time if you know who's going to win, could you please tell me, okay? I need the money. What about you, Miss Lionheart? Were you tempted to have a flutter?"

"No," Lilly said. "The only person I ever bet on is myself." She opened the lab door and rushed over to rescue Quetzee.

"Prrrtssz." Quetzee scrabbled his paws against the Plastech. "Prrrtssz."

"Sorry Quetzee." Lilly opened the cage, and he ran up her arms.

Missy gasped. "Are you sure you should let it do that? You know it's dangerous."

"Quetzee? Don't be silly, he's a sweetheart," Lilly said as the forgiving wee soul licked her face with his forked tongue. Once she was sure he was happy, Lilly turned her attention to the AW[30] to see if the dreadbeast had made it through the last hour or so intact.

It had. The greenish line on the monitor scrolled along with a nice steady rise and fall as Squidge reset the alarms, babbling excitedly. "Just think. Now we have almost finished with the dreadbeasts, we can make a dragon!"

"With three million pounds? I'd have thought thirty million would still be a little short of what we need to make a winged fire-breathing behemoth with deadly claws, and teeth the size of swords," Lilly replied. "But that's just me."

"Behemoth?" Squidge said. "I do not think we are making one of those."

---

30 Artificial Womb

Lilly sighed. "I just meant a dragon would be big. And expensive."

"I have a few ideas about that. We may have to cut a few corners, but it will still be lethal."

"Yes, that's what I was worried about," Missy muttered. "Not making a flying, fire-breathing, dragon lethal enough."

"Anyway," Lilly said artlessly, having thought of a way to get Squidge out of the room so she could check the rat experiment maps on his laptop. "I don't suppose you remembered to bring back Prof's book?"

Squidge's mouth dropped. He gave a little squeak of terror and rushed off to find out where Mr Big had left Prof's sketchbook.

Now was the perfect opportunity. She wandered over to Squidge's computer.

Someone yawned behind her.

"Oh." Lilly stifled a jump. "Missy. You're still here? You should go to bed. It's … a big day tomorrow."

"Good idea." Still yawning, Missy wandered out. The doors swung back and forth behind her.

Lilly listened impatiently as the sound of footsteps trailed off down the corridor. She opened Squidge's laptop … a few minutes should be enough. Typing in his password and quickly pulling up the fuzzy images from the echolocation experiment.

§

From: Security@MrBig.net.www.e
To: MrBig@MrBig.net.www.e
Subject: It's on.
Time: Dec 25, 21:51

Boss, are you there? She accessed the file. Again.

11sftm

To: Security@MrBig.net.www.e
From: MrBig@MrBig.net.www.e
Subject: It's on.
Time: Dec 25, 21:54

Good. Make sure your men are ready.

3sftm

§

Lilly rotated the picture on the screen. Yes, that thick fuzzy line represented the wall in front of the electrified exit. And there was another corridor leading toward it. A better way to get into the guard post. Then, if she managed to disable the guards and cross the electrified floor, there really weren't all that many twists and turns and guard posts after that. Easy. Except for the guards. And the floor. And the electrified water spraying down from the pipes.

She looked around the lab for inspiration. She wanted a gadget that could stun the guards and short-circuit the floor from a distance.

Squidge would be able to do it. Create a remote, or some kind of switch-flicking device …

But she couldn't trust Squidge. Not to escape. Could she?

No, she could only trust herself, and Quetzee. Quetzee was a pretty good remote – at least for lights. If only—

The doors opened and Squidge entered, carrying Prof's book as though it was a precious relic.

It was too late to close the computer, so Lilly settled for closing the incriminating file and opening an article Squidge had written about DNA folding.

It was most insightful. Would have saved a heap of time too.

"Oh that," Squidge said, looking over her shoulder. "Yes, maybe we did not take the laws of folding into consideration quite as much as we should have in the dreadbeasts. But I think we will have a workable critter as soon as we have sorted out a few bugs."

*Good luck with that*, she thought, pretending to be studying a solution. All she could think about was when she should make her move. The obvious time was tonight, in the wee hours of the morning – no, that was stupid, most of the people in here were up at that time. Around 7 am, would be better. Hopefully the guards would be under the weather after their all-night celebrations. The problem was if she was escaping tonight, it didn't leave much time for planning. Actually, no time for planning. Especially as Lilly needed to sleep if she was going to think straight.

"Night," she said to Squidge.

He shrugged and turned back to his computer. Quetzee, still upset from when she'd left him earlier, chittered as she stood up.

He'd calmed down by the time they got to her room, helpfully turning out the light several times before climbing on the bed.

Closing her eyes, Lilly almost let exhaustion carry her to sleep, before she remembered to set her alarm. Even then, she soon drifted into sweet dreams of living at home, where the only thing she had to worry about were exams.

Then the school bell rang.

Not the school bell! She sat bolt upright and reached for her alarm.

Not that either. No, it was the dreadbeast alarm.

So much for her day off.

So much for Christmas.

So much for escaping.

Lilly pulled on a dressing gown, grabbed a half asleep and quite grumpy snake-hybrid, and ran.

As Quetzee's increasingly long and painful claws dug into her shoulders she reflected that running to the lab was becoming rather a nasty habit. It was one of the many habits she intended to lose as soon as possible. *But not quite yet*, she thought, opening the lab door with trepidation.

•22•

# BETRAYED

As **Lilly entered the** lab, Quetzee stopped kneading her shoulders with his claws, jumped down, and rushed to the cages.

She ignored him and hurried over to Squidge, already hunched over his computer. "What is it this time?"

"The same," he replied, without looking up.

While Lilly got to work, Quetzee patrolled the reptiles for a while, before skidding to a halt and hissing at Esmeralda.

Esmeralda hissed back, head waving to and fro as the rest of her body coiled protectively around a clutch of freshly laid eggs.

"You should do something," Squidge said, distracted by the commotion.

"Squidge, stop fussing over Ezzy and her eggs. She's perfectly safe. We need to focus, and figure out a plan – preferably one that includes sleep. I'm tired of being called back to the lab for these emergencies."

"But it is so aggravating." Squidge thumped the extremely expensive and difficult to replace artificial womb. "This stupid thing is designed for mammals. Normally after sterilisation the amniotic fluid will cool sufficiently, but this dreadbeast cannot handle anything over 298 Kelvins."

"So what are we going to do?"

"There is nothing we can do. Not without introducing infection, or damaging the unit."

"We'll figure something," Lilly said with a poor attempt at cheeriness. "Come on, whatever it is, we can fix it. After all, we already did the hardest bit, the sequencing, and that was perfect."

Squidge screwed up his face as he adjusted his glasses. "We can not know for absolute certain. Not until we see the final product. Besides, I can make it more perfect, we just—"

A thud reverberated around the lab.

Squidge stopped. Mouth open, he pointed wordlessly at Quetzee, who having crashed into Ezzy's cage had righted himself groggily, and started to lick a stray patch of fur. "I told you, you should do something about that creature."

With her body still curled tightly around her eggs, Esmeralda hissed again. She reared and struck the Plastech with a clonk. Her head wobbled a little as she recovered, forked tongue stabbing the air angrily, neck stretched out high and stiff.

Quetzee resumed prowling, scrambling around the other side of the cage when Lilly tried to pick him up.

"Come on, Quetzee. You're only going to hurt yourself," Lilly called, but Quetzee just scampered off again to taunt Esmeralda, who hissed and launched another attack – her head crashing against the cage again.

Some of the other lab-animals joined in – shrieking, yowling, and scratching at their cages.

"Ovulating Octopoda! Quetzee, stop it right now," Lilly snapped and bent down, determined to gather him into her arms. Fluffy tail high in the air, he chittered angrily and jumped through her widespread arms. She sighed. "Stop being a brat. You can't eat Esmeralda or her eggs."

"Wretched creature," Squidge shouted, brandishing a micropipette at Quetzee. "First you eat my dreadbeast, and now you are terrorising Esmeralda's eggs."

"Eggs?! Wait a minute," Lilly said. "We've been so stupid, we could—"

Squidge jumped up. "Perfect. You brilliant, annoying creature!" He bent down as if to scoop up Quetzee, then veered sharply from Quetzee's bared fangs as they snapped shut.

Having made his point, although perhaps not the point he'd intended, Quetzee lifted his tail and ran up Lilly's arm. From the safety of her shoulder, he turned back to hiss at Squidge.

Lilly muttered under her breath. "You were just hungry, weren't you Quetzee?"

"I think we need to increase the repeats on intron FR92," Squidge said.

Lilly wasn't really listening. "Good idea," she replied, and waved him away. "Quetzee, you're hungry for live food, aren't you? I'm sure I can find something." The lab stores were full of everything they needed to feed almost every creature imaginable, so finding something for Quetzee shouldn't be that difficult.

Several mice and a guinea pig later, he fell asleep, snoring gently on a lab stool while Lilly got on with giving Squidge a hand. It was fascinating. She was learning more here than she ever would at university with stick-in-the-mud professors. She'd be almost sad to leave this place, and her team. Especially Squidge.

If only she could trust them. Rescue them too. But that wasn't an option. It was far too dangerous. Instead, she determined to use this moment to work harder than ever, so they – and this new batch of dreadbeasts – would have the best chance of living once she was gone. Soon she was so involved she forgot about her imminent escape, and the fast-passing time – until Squidge got up and paced the lab. He was debating loudly with himself the merits of various updated features. "Um," Lilly muttered. It was already 6 am! "I just need a quick nap."

Squidge nodded and yawned. "I will sleep later. You will have to cover for me then."

"That's fine," Lilly said, feeling a rising excitement to be off. She picked up the sleeping Quetzee, draped him around her shoulders, and walked briskly down the corridor, towards the cafeteria where Queen's, *I Want to Break Free* was pumping from the sound system.

As she neared, she passed signs the Christmas party had got a bit out of control; tinsel, streamers, mini-fireworks, a blackened hand chewed off at the wrist. Slumped on the floor right outside the cafeteria was a thug – a bottle of wine loosely grasped in his fingers.

A plan forming, Lilly knelt down and gently prised the wine off the man. "Bud … id … mine," the drunkard protested, turned over and started snoring.

Waving the bottle around in her best imitation of someone who didn't care about the damage of alcohol poisoning, Lilly weaved her way down the corridor. With everyone else looking worse for wear, she figured the appearance of a drunken person out of bounds, wouldn't be so unusual.

A group of revellers approached.

Lilly saw Deva amongst them and jumped. *Don't panic*, she told herself.

Deva pointed at her.

*Aortal arrhythmia, why now?*

"Lilshy," Deva slurred. "I shee you've brought your famoush beasht."

Lilly pretended to stumble. "Dringshki," she slurred, waving the bottle about and swaying unsteadily.

The revellers squinted nervously at Quetzee, and veered away, before resuming their revelry.

Soon the familiar crackling popping noise from the electrified floor told Lilly she was getting close. Maybe it was the Christmas celebrations, or perhaps simple luck, but nobody else passed by.

Slowly, quietly she opened the guardroom door and peered in, but it was hard to see much aside from flashes of light and someone, half in shadow, perched on a chair. There could be more. There should be more. *All or nothing*, she told herself, swallowing her courage and pushing the door open.

"I gotta presen' fer ewes," Lilly slurred, resisting an inexplicable urge to say *baa*. Could the guards even hear her over the racket made by the electrified floor – arcing, zapping and crackling behind them?

Continuing to wave the wine bottle erratically, she cased the room. Two guards lounged in uncomfortable wooden chairs, with an empty six-pack of beer beside them. They both looked bad, and smelt worse – with breath reminiscent of several breweries and a cheese factory. Even better, nobody was on the other side of the electrified walkway.

"Dringkee? Tha'll be nice," said one, holding his beer can out as if it were a mug, before losing his balance and tipping off the chair.

As he hit the ground, the walkway not so far behind his head erupted in pops and crackles of arcing electricity.

Had he tripped an alarm?

No. The noise was nothing more than mini-thunderclaps and extra water being shaken from the overhead pipes.

The other guard stood. "How about you go away. I don't think you should be—"

Lilly counter-offered. "Dringshki?" she asked, waving her bottle with an extra vigorous flourish so that it clonked the guard's head. The nasty hollow sound rang around the room.

"Oops." Lilly winced, and not just for show. That had to hurt. He slumped back into his chair with a heavy thud-crack of furniture. Double ouch. Still, now wasn't the time to fuss. If she didn't get across the floor before backup arrived, she'd be far worse off than a slightly-injured guard. Fortunately the floor wasn't as impassable as Mr Big might think.

Not because she'd created a gizmo like a *proper* spy. Although, thinking about it, in a way she had. She'd helped design Quetzee, seen his possibilities and trained him. Now, all she had to do was get him to run over the overhead water pipes, and flick off the switch for the floor. There was no one on the other side to stop him.

"Switch!" Lilly whispered pointing to the far wall.

Quetzee chittered excitedly, twisted out of her arms, and jumped to the floor. Lilly bit back a scream – if he rushed across the electrified metal he'd die! Fortunately, he turned and scampered back to the light switch at the doorway. He bashed it up and down, and looked at her expectantly.

Lilly shook her head. "Not that one."

Quetzee chirruped, tongue flicking in and out, head darting to and fro.

She ditched the wine bottle and grabbed him, climbed up a stool and placed him on the large central pipe. "Light switch, Quetzee. Over there."

"Prrrtssz," he called. After a moment, he ran along the water pipe highway that almost seemed made for him.

Heart in mouth, Lilly watched.

"*Switch*!" she hissed.

He jumped down. He batted the switch. Too many times. The floor was still crackling.

"*Light switch*!" Lilly was sweating with fear. What if he decided to run back along the floor now?

The guard she'd hit groaned.

The blue flashes stopped. The floor was safe. "Good boy. Stop. Come on, Quetzee. Shoulders."

Tail up, Quetzee rushed across the floor, and bounced up onto her shoulder. Lilly rewarded him with a tiny piece of bacon as she crossed the treacherous surface as fast as she could. In the middle of the metal floor plate, too late to go back, she heard a groan. What if a guard recovered in time to stop her? Why hadn't she taken the time to incapacitate them properly?

Quetzee mewled in her ear, restless, as if he sensed her unease.

Lilly looked back the way they had come. Nothing was moving. "Good boy, Quetzee," she said, trying to soothe him. "You're so clever."

Before she could make it to the other side of the plate, the door in front of her creaked open. She meant to rush forward and take whomever it was by surprise, but found herself skidding to a halt as Mr Big entered – Annie to his left, and Pinhead Pat to his right.

Lilly looked down, her feet were still several metres from the edge of the metal. She looked up, trying not to flinch at the self-satisfied smirk plastered across Mr Big's face. Her heart beat faster as she saw both men had guns trained on her. No, Mr Big didn't have a gun – it was a remote control.

Behind her, someone was moving. One of the guards – the one who'd fallen off his chair earlier – was now on his feet, twirling his gun around his finger, and obviously not nearly so drunk as she'd thought.

*Dendritic deception*[31]*! How am I going to explain this?* Lilly thought, before deciding on a classic. After all, it had

---

31 Dendrites: short, branched extensions on nerve cells that help receive and transmit messages. *VF*

appeared to work so well earlier. "Dringshkie?" she said, almost gargling what should have been a non-existent *g*, and holding up an empty hand – as she remembered she'd left the bottle behind.

"You don't fool me for a second, Miss Lionheart. It's been rather fun playing these games. But now, I think it's time for you to die."

"I'm not keen on that particular option," Lilly said, forgetting drunk and trying for an insouciant shrug. "How about you let me go instead?"

"Let you go? In this place, you know, it does all rather mean the same thing. Unfortunately, when I suggested it to Squidge earlier, he wasn't that keen. Wanted to keep you on for some reason. Pity. Still, he has been rather useful in telling me exactly what you've been up to."

"Oh." Lilly tried to ignore the cold sense of betrayal in her stomach. So she'd been right not to trust Squidge. Even so ...

Tongue flicking, Quetzee hissed at Mr Big, then glanced sideways at Annie, and daintily licked his lips. Annie mirrored the gesture in a distorted overly-large funhouse mirror kind of way; copious amounts of drool giving her chops an added ripple effect.

Mr Big didn't seem to notice. "You see Squidge's little maps were out of date. I only leave them scattered about the place for people silly enough to think they can escape. It's much more efficient to have troublemakers come here, rather than for me to go to the bother of finding them. So, go on, take a look around."

Lilly took a deep breath and half walked, half ran off the metal floor and through the open doorway. Where the map had said there'd be a choice of three corridors, concrete walls and cell-sized cubes of blackened glass confronted Lilly.

"This section has been rebuilt into a jailhouse. Now do you think this place is secure enough? Even for you?"

For a second, Lilly thought about applauding, such was the pride in his voice. She stopped, hands poised in front of her.

"Yes, it is perfect, isn't it?" Mr Big gushed, not just for her benefit, but for anyone within a half-mile radius. "And after a while, any little troublemakers I decide to let live, forget about such silly little concepts as freedom, and begin to figure out how to make their stay more comfortable, and less … tortuous … if you understand my meaning."

Lilly nodded dumbly, staring at the line of concrete and glass cells.

"You know, I'm almost disappointed. After all, you were recommended by two very remarkable people. I believe you've met?"

He pressed a button on the remote and one of the walls of darkened glass shimmered. "I've been dying to introduce you."

Somehow Lilly knew who it was before they'd even appeared. Even so, it was a shock as the all-too-familiar faces peered back at her. Her mother's long dark hair was almost scraggly, her father – less than perfectly groomed. Not at all the same people she remembered admonishing her for being a little dishevelled after that stupid New York marathon.

She told herself that it could be worse, that at least her parents were alive, and Mr Big hadn't killed them like he'd threatened to. However, there was a part of her that couldn't help but be disappointed these heroes from her childhood had allowed themselves to be captured. At least now some of the cryptic notes she'd received made some kind of sense. Maybe. It all depended on *when* they'd been captured.

"Mum? Dad?"

"Ah, I don't think so." Mr Big said with evident relish. "They *said* that they were your parents. Problem is, they're not. Quite sad. It's a silly lie, and rather easy to disprove. I'm surprised you haven't worked it out already."

"What!?" Lilly said.

Mr Big smiled wider.

She clamped her mouth shut. Emotion was exactly what he wanted.

"If I'm right – and I'm always right," Mr Big continued. "They killed your parents when you were hardly more than a babe." He licked his lips. "And Lilly you're actually the daughter of the now dead, Dr Frankenstein the Third."

"No!" Lilly's mother cried.

"Ridiculous!" her father blustered. "Lilly, you have to—"

Lilly could feel her face fall as Mr Big grinned wider still. "Isn't that delicious?" Mr Big said. He pushed a button and their protests were silenced – although their mouths still moved. Her father's neck strained as his face turned a very un-spy-like red.

"Sweeter and sweeter," Mr Big gloated. "They wanted you. Either that, or someone wanted them to train you. But why? And how did your résumé end up on my desk?

"In order to discover the answers to my questions, I thought I'd invite them to stay here a while. Unfortunately, they've been about as informative as you have—

"Don't look at me with your mouth open. I thought you were a genius, girl."

Lilly, realising that somewhere in this one-sided conversation her mouth had fallen open, snapped it shut.

Mr Big smiled and idly scratched the ruff on Annie's neck. "And why do you think that they decided to teach you that particular branch of science? The genetics and biochemistry of hybridisation is hardly a mainstream university subject."

Lilly's childhood came back in flashes – the endless spy training and martial arts, punctuated only by a few pleasant hours spent in the lab. Cherished times.

"Are you saying all they were doing was training some dupe for a mission. A fall guy?"

"Exactly." Mr Big grinned. He banged on the glass. "You did hear that, didn't you?"

"It's not like that," they shouted at her. She couldn't hear them – but it was basic lip-reading 101. She didn't bother trying to figure out if they were lying. As spies, that was their job, and they'd always been far too good at it.

Lilly turned and walked away, back to her room.

"Just wait!" Pinhead called. He handed Lilly two cotton swabs, and unlocked the door.

§

Dear Diary

I've not had much time for diaries. Besides, lately there's been nothing much to say – until now. Mr Big, I know you read these. Don't think I'm going to fall for your lies that easily, or thank you for any of this. Finding out you are adopted is one thing, and I'd always suspected it, but this? You have gone too far.

It was awful. My parents stood there, the muscles in their cheeks working furiously, but not saying anything. Not after the first couple of attempts, when Pat gave them both split lips for their trouble.

I didn't say a word, either. Besides, anything I said wouldn't amount to much – except that it might be taken the wrong way.

Life's like that, very simple and extremely complicated all at the same time. Are the people in lockup my biological parents? And if so, what should I do about it?

Either way, I can't escape and leave them here. They would be killed. And a rescue attempt would be suicidal. And for what? Biological parents? Devoted foster parents or manipulative agents? Or both, or all three? I'm not even sure I want to know. Until I do, I've put the samples on ice. It's not like I don't have all the time in the world to find out.

So that leaves me stuck in this fashion-free zone, with the Spring Catalogue of Evil being the chic highlight of the year. But if I am to be stuck, I might as well make the most of it. The embryos are implanted, and the baby dreadbeasts are beginning to wriggle inside the shells.

At least Mr Big, for all his bluster, doesn't want to kill me... yet.

§

To: Security chiefsftm@MrBig.net.www.e
From: MrBig@MrBig.net.www.e
Subject: We need to make an example
Time: Dec 26, 8:45

Security 1 informs me those blasted spies are gone. I don't know how, but they blasted through that cage and the concrete bunker wall. This disaster is going to take weeks to clean up. Its about thyme we showed to everybody what happens to spy's in this plaice. Set it up. Now. And I'll go see that Miss L.

Your Boss and Overlord
Mr Big

§

To: MrBig@MrBig.net.www.e
From: Securitychiefsftm@MrBig.net.www.e
Subject: We need to make an example
Time: Dec 26, 8:59

Didn't we just do that? Isn't that why we killed the two techies outside the cafeteria? And showed Miss Lionheart the prison?

sftm

# •23•

# DOWN A RABBIT HOLE

LILLY WOKE WITH A sickening feeling. Something was wrong, and it wasn't the rasping tongue licking her face. "Quetzee? If that's you, quit it."

She rolled over. Maybe it was some kind of weird dream turned nightmare, triggered by too much rich Christmas food, and an overactive imagination. Quetzee licked her again, and she blinked her eyes open to the horrible realisation it was all true. Yes, Quetzee was real, and that was good – but so was last night's humiliating ordeal.

One moment she found herself making elaborate plans to rescue her so-called parents, the next she wanted to escape and leave them to rot in their cell. It was doing her head in. And what made it worse was that this was exactly what Mr Big wanted.

But there are things you do to survive, even if you're already half dead from lack of sleep. Getting up is one of them. Especially as Quetzee wasn't planning to give her any choice. "Prrrtssz," he complained, bashing her face with a paw.

Squidge walked into the lab and looked Lilly up and down. "Gosh you look a mess," he said. "You should brush your hair or something."

"Thanks." Lilly smiled in a way most people would recognise as sarcastic. She scowled and ran her fingers through her hair.

"That is alright." Squidge returned the smile artlessly. "I heard you tried to escape last night."

"I needed a new outfit," she said, looking down at the crumpled overalls she'd thrown on, and wondering at how far her standards had fallen.

"Oh," Squidge said as if the need for a new outfit explained everything.

"There, there," he said stiffly. "Do not worry, everyone tries to escape once. I did. But then I came straight back again."

"You never told me why you did that," Lilly said.

"Bored," he replied. As if this explained everything – and maybe it did. Or maybe he was just an accomplished traitor.

"How terrible," she said. "A little boredom must be so much worse than being stuck inside here, trying to create Prof's mutant creatures for a crazed psychopath."

"Yes," Squidge said. "It would be terrible. Fortunately my creatures are genetically *designed*, and not old-school mutants, or I would be extremely embarrassed."

"Yeah. Whatever." Lilly picked at a thread escaping from her cuff. "I don't suppose you'd tell me how to get out?"

"You need a new outfit that badly?"

"Absolutely. And I also need to get help for some prisoners in the detention facility past the northern perimeter."

"A detention facility? Past the Northern Perimeter? Are you sure?"

Lilly sighed. "No, I just fell down a rabbit hole. Any minute now I'm going to be asked out on a very important date."

Squidge looked at her blankly. "A rabbit hole? Around here?"

Lilly rolled her eyes. "Oh, silly me. Yes, maybe I'm wrong.

Maybe I'll wake up and find out that there are no packs of cards nearby, and my parents are in fact being held in your old escape route, now turned detention centre in the North Wing."

He looked Lilly up and down. "Are you being sarcastic?"

Lilly scowled at Squidge, grabbed a bunch of readouts, and pointedly ignored him. Maybe this was just an act. Or maybe, just maybe, she hadn't been completely deceived and outwitted by the boy after all. But she still felt betrayed. It didn't have to make sense. Did it?

Squidge stood and stared at her. "You know," he said after a while. "People die escaping. I would not want you to die. It would be most inconvenient."

"That's an odd thing to say. How else did Mr Big know I was escaping if you didn't tell him?"

"I—" Squidge started but never finished the sentence because at that moment Missy walked in.

Squidge put his finger to his lips.

"Yeah," she muttered. "You're my best buddy. Like I'd believe that."

"Oh, Lilly, I have something to tell you," Missy said looking askance at Squidge before giving him a wide berth. She took Lilly by the arm and whispered, "Us girls should stick together. Maybe grab a drink."

It seemed strange behaviour for Missy, but Lilly didn't much feel like working, so they took weak-as-dishwater coffee from the store room, and went and watched the menagerie. It was nice to see all the animals living their lives in ignorant peace.

The room became less peaceful as soon as Quetzee hopped off her shoulder and started running back and forth.

"You have to be more careful," Missy said. "Around here you can't be too cautious about who you talk to."

Lilly nodded. "I thought I was being very careful. Things

around here are crazy."

Missy dropped her voice conspiratorially, "There aren't that many girls in this operation. We need to look out for each other."

"Yes," Lilly said absently, watching Quetzee slinking across the ground, pretending to ignore the lions as they shook their manes, wrinkled their noses and snarled back at him. Even a roar of protest only had him skittering back a couple of feet, before tipping back onto his hind legs, hissing just like the squirrel-snake he was, and sending the lab animals into paroxysms of fright.

The girls jumped up as Pat kicked the door open to let Mr Big into the lab. "Right," Mr Big said levelling his gun at her. "Where's this motherless dreadbeast you've been making then?"

"Um," Lilly said, trying to stifle the fact that she'd nearly jumped out of her skin.

He waved his gun. "The incubator is broken, isn't it?"

Lilly nodded. She didn't mean to. She shook her head. It was hard to think straight looking down the barrel of a gun.

"I should never have listened to you or that Squidge," he spat at Missy. "You're both too soft."

Lilly took a pointless step backward. "I ... Uh ... " How could she explain things, when she didn't exactly know his problem? As she floundered, knowing death was just the twitch of a finger away, the door flung open and Squidge burst in.

"Walk away, boy." Mr Big waved his gun. "She's dead. Should have killed her last night. She's infiltrated this operation for the WWWOS. You helped them, didn't you?"

What was the man talking about now? And to whom? Her? Squidge? Missy? Lilly's head hurt with his special brand of crazy.

Biting his lip, Squidge turned to walk away.

“Squidge!” Lilly yelled desperately. He might be a slim hope, but he was all she had.

He shook his head and beckoned to Missy. They both disappeared behind the door.

“Squidge,” Lilly said softly, knowing he couldn’t hear her. And wouldn’t do anything about it even if he could. Otherwise he’d have executed a bold and brilliant rescue plan a long time ago. But she had to wonder, what was the point of being a genius if you were only going to do the sensible thing?

•24•

# WHEN YOUR WHOLE WORLD IS BLACK

EYES CLOSED, LILLY WENT to a very dark place. Not red hot, like anger. Something more frightening. An emptiness that took hold of her and wouldn't let go.

"Is there something you'd like to confess before the end?" Mr Big asked.

Lilly opened her eyes, letting go of the bloody blackness behind her eyelids, and embraced the bloody blackness that had become her life. "You think your boy Squidge runs the lab? You think I did nothing?" Lilly spat at Mr Big.

Pat raised an eyebrow, and Quetzee stopped swaggering by the monkeys, and slunk behind a cage of broody quails.

How could Mr Big do this now, when her plans were all in hand? Well, obviously not the part where she'd failed to escape and found out her parents had been captured, but the dreadbeast experiment itself was finally starting to look more than just promising. But … if he'd wanted to kill her for that, he could have done it last night. Much simpler.

Which meant Mr Big still wanted something. Something Squidge didn't have. The reason he'd hired her in the first place.

"You think *Squidge* would have managed to execute my brilliant plan?"

"What brilliant plan?" he said warily.

"You have a whole clutch of snake eggs filled with dreadbeast embryos thanks to me. *I* am what makes this program. *Me*. You think if I was a nark I'd have stuck around this long, with you pointing a gun at my head every five minutes? But, before I die, I need to know one thing, since I've been too busy to check. Last night. Did you lie to me?"

He shook his head in confusion.

Jaw set, Lilly repeated the question. "Last night. Did you lie to me about my parents?"

He laughed. "No, that would be stupid. You have all the evidence you need."

Lilly bit her lip. She hadn't even looked at the cotton swabs, let alone tested them, but that wasn't the point. "So why did you bring me here in the first place? Because I'm a genius, or because you thought I was a spy you could feed false information to? What exactly *were* you expecting me to do?"

"Give up your contacts."

Lilly opened her mouth.

Mr Big's face turned red. Redder. "Perhaps you need a little demonstration of what happens to spies."

"Lucky I am a scientist then, isn't it?"

Pat smiled. "I think it's time to show Miss Lionheart some of our aquatic wildlife."

"This way, Miss." Mr Big's words were accompanied by a sarcastic bow. "Since you're determined to live a while longer, let's go and visit the shark tank. By the way – lots of dreadbeasts – that's a true work of genius. I can't wait until they hatch."

"Neither can I," Lilly muttered. "Neither can I."

"I think you've won your way into Mr Big's heart," Pat joked.

Nobody laughed.

Silently, they walked into a swanky section of the lair she'd never been to. Alligator-skin couches lined the walls of a small amphitheatre surrounding a pool. Near the pool, a tall, dark haired young man was ringed by minions throwing punches. Were they sparring? It all seemed rather light-hearted as the young man toasted their arrival with a martini and dropped an opponent.

Mr Big raised his hand in a half wave. "Very good, Jimmy. Thanks for training my guys so well. Now I think it's time for you to die. We can't have spies hanging around here forever you know."

"What?" the young man responded, laughing. "Me? A spy? Never."

"What are you waiting for? Kill him," Mr Big told the minions. "Let's see if you've learnt something."

Before any of the minions sparring him moved as much as half a step, the young man grabbed a thug by the legs, and swung. The thug screamed as his body hurtled around in a tight arc, knocking minions off their feet, before he was released to careen into the pool. The splash greeted with evil laughter from Mr Big.

The water roiled and twisted, as a shark dragged the minion under. Lilly looked away from the sight of crimson blood in the blue water.

"I told you to watch," Mr Big said, forcing her jaw around.

Another shark snapped its jaws around the body, tearing him apart as it surged out of the water. It swam off, clutching half the minion's torso in its bloody jaws.

"Wasn't that fun?" Mr Big smiled and signalled to Pat. "Now, keep watching, the next bit is even more important."

Pat approached the suave spy, "Time to get serious." The other minions melted away at his approach.

"Man on man," the spy said, saluting Pat with his glass. "How sporting."

Pat didn't say anything, he simply faked a punch and roundhouse kicked the young man into the pool.

To give him credit, the dark haired young man never let go of his drink – bravely swimming to the edge of the pool, before screaming, and disappearing in a tumult of blood-frothed bubbles.

"Spies. Stupid. I would never be a spy. You should believe me."

"Maybe we do," Mr Big said. "Or maybe we think that you'll change your mind when you discover the truth. Go and check, will you? Pat, make sure she does, will you."

Pat frowned and flicked an imperceptible speck of dust from his suit. "Yes, sir."

§

To: MrBig@MrBig.net.www.e
From: Securitychiefsftm@MrBig.net.www.e
Subject: We need to make an example.
Time: Dec 26, 10:04

Why do you continue to let her live? She's been an awful lot of trouble for not much result.

chiefsftm

§

To: Securitychiefsftm@MrBig.net.www.e
From: MrBig@MrBig.net.www.e
Subject: I should make the egg sample out of you.
Time: Dec 26, 10:17

How could you lose two assets from a securely locked sell?

We can't afford for Squidge to get upset and lose his focus now. So don't even think about arranging an accident. At least not yet. Not until she has drawn out a few more spy's within my network. Besides I would like to think that she can be maid to sea things our way. And you have to admit – lots of dreadbeasts. That's the work of a true genius. I cant wait until they hatch.

Your Boss and Overlord,
Mr Big

.

# •25•

# THE HATCHING

LILLY PULLED THE DNA swabs out from storage, hesitating one final time.

What did it matter if they were her biological parents or not? Except for the niggling fear she'd had since she'd arrived, that somehow she'd been deliberately placed into the hands of the WWWOE. If so, her intense training, and her parents' insistence hard work was the cure for everything, could be taken in a new, and very sinister light. Which meant Missy might have been right when she'd said, "Your parents lied. And they don't sound very nice either." And that smarted.

Was she nothing more than a chess piece, raised to play a tiny role as a cog in the endless game of WWWOE vs WWWOS tit for tat?

Knowing her emotions were being played by Mr Big, Lilly took a moment to think about his behaviour. Something was up, and she was sick of being played by – everybody.

But she had to know …

Soon she had the results she was dreading. Her parents were no relation to her. At all.

Instead of being angry, she decided to play it cool. She'd been lied to, yes, but at least now she had the facts. It would do no good to allow herself to be baited into jumping to conclusions, or rushing into finding more answers she could not deal with. So instead of throwing tantrums, or making demands, Lilly did what she'd been trained to do, and threw herself into her work.

Squidge, already caught up in dragon fever, left her to complete the final dreadbeast tweaks by herself and replace the snake embryos with dreadbeasts. It was a nerve wracking couple of days. Especially after all the lies she'd told. The dreadbeasts, weren't nearly as far along as she'd said.

When she did at last get them into the incubator, she gathered the team around to congratulate them all on this little success. And to let them congratulate her. Now it was just a matter of time for the dreadbeasts to hatch. Or not. A horrible possibility that hung as thickly over the lab as the smell of the nearby menagerie.

The dragon project, crazy though it was, quickly became fun. Lilly spent a week working on how to best structure dragon bone. Bat's bone, even bird bone and dinosaur prototypes were put through various stressors, and came up short of what was required for such a large flying creature. Getting the bone, and teeth, lightweight and still strong enough was proving a real challenge.

And while she was doing that, she'd be interrupted by explosions as Brian tested incendiaries against various organic and non-organic materials. Mostly because it was fun helping him out. Missy thought so too, but she was more focussed on how to make improvements to the structure of the menagerie itself. Not just for the dragons, but their other dangerous creatures, especially the lions and dinosaurs, and also containment for the dreadbeasts, when – and if – they hatched.

And then one morning – after Lilly had let a piranha-toothed guinea-pig out of its cage for Quetzee's breakfast, and Brian had accidentally caught fire to a lab bench – Lilly turned on the candling[32] light to check the dreadbeast eggs. She gasped delightedly as she saw the red-veined shadows of embryos were moving – waggling their heads back and forth.

"Come quick!" she yelled at Squidge.

Squidge ignored her, and Quetzee hissed and bounded away in annoyance as his breakfast mop of fur squeaked and scooted across the floor in front of her feet.

Brian and Missy, having only just arrived, stared at her, bleary eyed and uncomprehending, as she danced around the lab. "The dreadbeasts are moving!"

Joyfully, she dragged her co-workers over to the incubator and flicked the switch. Light shone through the eggs, and lit up the ghostly red embryos, so they could clearly see them waggling their thin legs and diamond-shaped heads within the shells.

Brian and Missy rushed over to congratulate her, while Squidge shrugged and went back to designing the dragon as if his life wasn't on the line at all. Thrilled the dreadbeasts were doing so well, Lilly began checking the eggs every spare minute …

Four days later, her anticipation was rewarded as the first leathery shell was pierced from within.

Should she help free the creature within? Should she wait? Lilly was caught in indecision as the egg tooth on the creature's snout very slowly ripped open the leathery shell. The moment the wedge-shaped snakehead emerged, slime trailing down its fangs, Lilly squealed with delight.

Missy squealed too, although the sound wasn't exactly one of delight.

---

32 candling: using a bright light to see the embryo within an egg

For once Lilly didn't complain, she was too busy jumping up and down as the creature's eight legs emerged, two at a time – and once they had a firm grip on the bench, pulled a fat abdomen the size of a golf ball out of the shell.

The boys were more reserved, watching from a couple of paces back, until Quetzee nosed in, tail high.

"No," Squidge said firmly, scooping the hatchling out of Quetzee's reach.

"Watch out!" Lilly said.

"Huh?" Squidge looked up, distracted as the dreadbeast raised poison-dripping fangs – and bit him.

"Ow!" Squidge shrieked, clutching his arm. "Not again."

Again? Well, he was kind of right, Lilly thought. The boy was always getting bit one way or another. She gathered Quetzee into her arms, and dumped him unceremoniously into a Plastech cage to howl. Squidge, already noticeably pale, pulled out a vial of antivenin and injected himself.

More dreadbeasts hatched. Soon they were everywhere. Even as newborns, all of ten centimetres long, they had a knack for climbing vertical surfaces, before jumping down to the floor on trails of spider silk, and legging it.

Lilly and Brian rounded up eight of the critters.

And though she knew she shouldn't get overly attached, she started naming them. Lightning was so fast she only caught him when he doubled back toward her. Fang threatened to bite Melissa who screamed and ran off. Skitter clattered across the table, and Chalky had the cutest white-tipped legs.

While Brian was safely caging Runt, the last dreadbeast to hatch, Lilly counted twelve ruptured eggshells.

Twelve? It was hard to think with Quetzee yowling and calling from his cage. She counted again. "Aberrant arachnids!" Where were the other four?

She rescued Quetzee.

Released, he stopped his howling and dashed up Lilly's shoulders, calling "prrrt prrrt." He kept on calling as she continued her frantic search for the missing dreadbeasts. No sign. How was she going to explain letting four dangerous critters out into the lab? Mr Big would kill her. Again.

Then she stopped panicking and looked about the lab. Although she was desperately looking for the dreadbeasts, no one else seemed to have noticed any were missing. Brian was still bailing the last dreadbeast into the cage, hindered by a slightly wobbly Squidge. Missy had climbed onto a lab stool, and was pretending to look for lab equipment on the top shelf. "Um, is it over?" she asked hopefully.

"Ah, not quite yet," Lilly said, insouciantly sweeping all the empty shells into a biohazard container.

Squidge, pale as he was, rang Mr Big with the exciting news that the dreadbeasts had finally hatched. She held her breath. Was he going to say anything about the missing ones? Did he even know about them?

He was trying to say something. It sounded important. Maybe he'd noticed them scamper off? Lilly held her breath, expecting any moment to discover she was in a world of trouble – but Squidge wasn't saying anything, he was gasping. Clutching at his throat with one hand, he fumbled in his pocket with the other.

"Squidge!" Lilly yelled as he tumbled to the ground. "Not again!"

## •26•

# THE ISSUE

SPITTLE FOAMED AROUND SQUIDGE'S mouth. He was going to give everyone in the room nightmares – if this wasn't a nightmare already. Lilly pinched herself, and pulled herself out of her daze.

Before he'd fallen, had Squidge been fumbling in his pocket for more antivenin?

"Masticating mitochondria!" She knelt down by his side and emptied his pockets of paper, wires, tubes, an empty vial of antivenin – and an epi-pen.

Of course.

"Missy!" Lilly called. "Brian?"

But Missy and Brian remained frozen.

Probably for the best. She'd been about to ask them to find the missing dreadbeasts – but that would've given away the fact the creatures were missing in the first place.

Best to just focus.

She applied the epi-pen to Squidge's arm, and, as soon as he was stable, bundled him up in an old blanket. Calm. Warm. Safe. No panic.

While she'd been occupied with matters of life and death, Missy had slipped out of the lab. Typical. Poor thing just didn't have the constitution to be a lab assistant. But Brian had come over to look after Squidge, so now at last she could search for the missing dreadbeasts.

... nothing ...

Slowly, she walked back to her desk, defeated. With much biting of her pen, she began to write in her notes: "Four deceased dreadbeasts. Survival-rate two thirds. No obvious abnormalities. Dreadbeasts have already demonstrated expression of the genes associated with venom, spider silk, and the adhesive setae[33] of gecko feet."

If she took some time to clean cages, maybe she'd find a dreadbeast, and if not, at least her charges would be well cared for. Best not to think about what would happen to them when she escaped – if she ever did.

While she was scrubbing Lilly didn't find any escaped dreadbeasts. But behind the small rodent section, she did notice two discarded dreadbeast exoskeletons caught on the bars of an empty rat cage. There was no sign either had died, just their cast-off external shells scintillating under the lab lighting – hard, cracked and very empty.

Carefully, Lilly disposed of them, a part of her happy her escaped dreadbeasts were growing well. As she went to check on the others, she couldn't help but wonder if this unexpected turn could be played to her advantage. No. There was no way this would be anything but trouble. She should say something now. Definitely, before this got out of hand, and the dreadbeasts became dangerous. But somehow, she couldn't bring herself to tell anyone. What if they wanted to hunt the escaped dreadbeasts down and kill them? What if? No.

Lilly walked over to the cage of captured dreadbeasts and smiled. They were perfect. And they seemed content, if a little hungry, as they scampered up and down the cage. She

33 Stiff hairs or bristles

added more beetles and lizards in the hope they, like their wild counterparts, would moult soon.

Quetzee watched on with interest and the occasional "prrrtssz," as the dreadbeasts began to hunt the new prey. Skitter ran back and forth over the cage, chased by Lightning. Tuffy, a previously unnamed dreadbeast received her name after picking a fight with her brothers and sisters over a gecko, and winning. Crunch got his from his eating habits. And Scratch got hers from the tiny white streak across her carapace.

After all the dreadbeasts had been named, and were well past their first moult, Mr Big came to gloat over the dreadbeasts. "Congratulations! And where are all my little killers?" he said, his entourage swaggering in after him. Lilly ushered everyone over to the cage where the dreadbeasts were piled in a heap on top of each other, like tiny, bloated, spidery kittens.

Mr Big's grin soon turned into a frown. "I thought they'd be more – I don't know ... scary. Right now they're about as frightening as mice," he scoffed. "Or that cat-squirrel of yours."

Lilly shook her head in disbelief. Quetzee was a snake-squirrel hybrid! And the dreadbeasts were just as dangerous. Surely Mr Big must know that? Especially after one had almost killed Squidge moments after hatching. The poor boy was hunched over his computer right now, still deathly pale and struggling to sit up, as he pored through his meticulous notes.

"Miss Lionheart, these dreadbeasts of yours are tiny. When will they get bigger? Fiercer? More dangerous?"

Lilly opened and closed her mouth a couple of times, lost for words.

Squidge looked up from his computer screen. "Time will

make them bigger," he said in an offhand way. No surprise there. In his new found passion to solve the dragon fire-breathing conundrum, Squidge could think of little else. What was life and death compared to a fascinating logic puzzle? Lilly quickly glanced at the screen, and sure enough it displayed the combustibility profiles of several different types of organic liquids.

"Yes," Lilly agreed. "Time will make them bigger."

If anything, Mr Big's frown deepened.

Perhaps a little exaggeration? "They will be huge. Real soon. Just you wait."

"I'm not a patient man, and neither is my competition," Mr Big muttered. "Fix it fast, or my *Spring Collection* will be ruined."

Not exactly the reaction Lilly might have hoped for. Given that his happiness kept her and her team alive, she would have to convince him her dreadbeasts were dangerous. The only problem was deciding what sort of creature, or creatures, she should pit them against. What was big enough, and scary enough, to impress Mr Big?

§

*Dear Diary*

*One of the newly born dreadbeasts almost killed Squidge and Mr Big doesn't think it is dangerous enough. I cannot believe it.*

*At least training Quetzee is fun. And I feel safer here with him to protect me. I always know I'm safe when he's around. His sweet nature and dangerous venom, make him the perfect bodyguard. Two amazing successes. So now all we have to do is scale things up and make a dragon. It will take a while to iron out some of the kinks. Even Squidge understands just how tricky that dragon is going to be to design. It might take a while.*

*Still, nothing good is ever easy.*

§

To: Miss Lionheart and Squidge.
From: Your Boss and Overlord
BCC: Security
Time: Jan 10, 9:02

Subject: Re: We need to make an example.
I am not impressed. So one of them bit Squidge, so Watt? Squidge gets bit by nearly every animal in here. Your teem has ten days to organza's a demonstration to prove how dangerous the dreadbeasts are. None of this flow chart, science gobbledegook. A reel test of skill, or I'll set my Annie on the lot of you.

Your Boss and Overlord,
Mr Big.

## •27•

# GREED

THE LAB DOORS BURST open. Mr Big. Yet again. "Ah, there you are, little Miss Lionheart," he said with a false bonhomie that made Lilly's teeth itch.

At least he didn't have Annie, just the two zombies, Basher and Veins, trailing along behind him. Both were still looking worse for wear from their fight with The Machine. Basher's face had been sewn shut from his nose to the bottom of his right ear.

Mr Big smiled. Something Basher wouldn't be doing again for a while – if ever. "I think it's about time you showed me around the menagerie to explain some of the changes you've been making."

"No problem," she lied. Reluctantly Lilly closed the tRNA simulation she'd been running – clamping down hard on the urge to sigh.

"But first, how are my *little* dreadbeasts going?" Mr Big needled.

Refusing to be baited, Lilly smiled. "They're growing so fast we're hardly keeping up with their demand for food." She took him over to their cage, relieved Quetzee wasn't nosing around. She hated to think how Mr Big might react to some of his antics.

He peered inside and grunted noncommittally. "Two hands high is hardly impressive."

"It's only been a week."

"And your obnoxious little bundle of fur?"

Lilly bit her tongue. She'd put him right, but Mr Big didn't really need to know her *little bundle of fur* was killing quite so many animals in his menagerie – even a few of the larger animals had turned up *mysteriously*[34] sick, sporting rather distinctive puncture marks.

"So," Mr Big said, clapping his hands together loud enough to not only get Veins and Basher jumping to attention, but also wake half the creatures in the lab, and send them scuttling away from the bars of their cages in high dudgeon. "Now it's time for you to show me the menagerie."

This time Lilly really did allow herself a sigh. After all, Mr Big would never hear it over all the hissing and rustling of animals.

Mr Big arched an eyebrow before ushering her through the door as if he were a gentleman – and not just someone who would rather have his enemies in front of him. "I heard there have been a number of … *accidents* … animals going missing?"

"Who could possibly have said that?" Lilly asked. "Squidge? A snooping Dr Deathless? Brian or Melissa? Unlikely. Did they even have the brains for it? Maybe … definitely. And Brian had been acting rather strangely since he'd lost his arm.

"Young lady, you know that I have my own sources."

"You mean them?" Lilly pointed at the cameras-eyes on bloated silver cushions floating toward them and attracted by the animals kicking up a fuss. "Anyway," Lilly said, changing tack. "If you care to check the animals, you will see they are

34 After we'd lost two ponies and a bulldog, administering Quetzee's antivenin became standard practice. *LL*

all healthy, and their cages are far more secure than in the past."

"Yes, I know. Your changes have been terribly expensive."

"Less expensive than losing irreplaceable creatures," Lilly insisted. "You'll notice we've left some of the smaller specimens back in the lab to increase live food production."

"Whatever. Shall we get to the point? I need to find some decent adversaries for these dreadbeasts of yours, because I need a proper demonstration before I can release my entries for the Spring Catalogue. I don't want any of those runts embarrassing me on the day. There's a lot of money riding on it."

As Mr Big and the zombies walked past the cages, the animals fretted – whining and yowling and pacing nervously. Highly strung creatures, they didn't seem to like these intruders at all. But, Mr Big, idiot that he was, seemed to be impressed. Especially by the roaring lions. "Now, those, Lilly – those are real predators. Not like that bundle of fur you're always coddling."

Lilly crossed her fingers, so far Quetzee had enough sense to stay hidden. Setting animals up to fight was odious. It was inhumane. A part of her job she absolutely detested. Still, so long as she could keep Quetzee and most of the animals safe, she had to make the best of a bad situation.

"Hmm," Mr Big muttered to himself. "All those dinosaurs are a little OTT, and besides, my minions betting against dinosaurs? I don't think so. But the lions there, they'll be perfect. Unless you have something else I should see?"

Lilly shook her head, the quicker he was out of here, the quicker she could get back to work.

It didn't work as well as she'd hoped. Mr Big didn't leave, instead he stuck about, wandering about and saying the first thing that popped into his head. As he passed the pterodactyls he muttered, "I don't like those flying things, their teeth aren't big enough." Then he scrutinised a troupe of spider monkeys. "Those hairy ape things don't seem very scary to me."

"I didn't create them." Lilly shrugged. It really wasn't her place to re-assure him about just how dangerous some of these animals could be, or for that matter to tell him the difference between apes and monkeys.

At last he wandered out of the menagerie, mumbling something Lilly couldn't quite catch about his plans for the upcoming fight. "Good riddance, senescent simians[35]," she muttered as the zombies trailed off after Mr Big.

Before hurrying back to the lab, Lilly stopped to admire the dreadbeasts. How dare Mr Big accuse them of being too small? It was only seven days after hatching, and they'd more than tripled in size. Even Squidge had been delighted with their progress. She put a rat the size of a small cat into their cage, and within moments it was happily being consumed by the whole tribe. It wouldn't be long before they were capable of much more. Still annoyed, she went to tell Squidge, but he wasn't interested at all in the upcoming fight. He was too busy pacing the room and shaking his head. "A dragon might be just a little bit harder than I thought. Fire-proof mucous membranes may not be possible using traditional methods."

Lilly could have told him that weeks ago. But she kept quiet. Squidge was too important to upset. He was such a whizz, she was beginning to wonder if there might be a chance for his ambitious vision of a real, live dragon to actually work. And not just because she wanted it to.

§

To: HR@MrBig.net.wwe
From: MrBig@MrBig.net.www.e

---

35 senescent – a characteristic of old age and, or a cell that no longer divides. Simian – resembling a monkey or ape. *VF*

CC: Lab2staff@MrBig.net.www.e
Subject: Dreadbeast Trail
Date: Jan 17, 20:21

Just to be sporting and even out the numbers, please ensure I have an extra lion ready for the 28th of January. After all a hole litter of dreadbeasts is rather cheating.

Your Boss and Overlord,
Mr Big

§

To: MrBig@MrBig.net.www.e
From: HR@MrBig.net.wwe
CC: Lab2staff@MrBig.net.www.e
Subject: Dreadbeast Trial
Date: Jan 17, 20:27

It is my pleasure, no, my prerogative to obtain this beast for you. My algorithms are here to serve.

Sincerely,
*VF Your virtual slave at HR*

§

Increasingly fond of her new charges, Lilly took to giving them runs out of their cage. But only when Quetzee was off on one of his hunting trips, just in case he decided to get jealous. They loved the attention, pushing up against her legs with shrill peeps and demanding to be stroked and fussed as she rubbed their carapaces with an oiled cloth until they shone. She also loved the way it brought out Scratch's streak, and Tuffy's playful side as he rolled around on the floor demanding attention.

As the dreadbeasts grew, they became more and more capable hunters, working together with a remarkable amount of social integration. Tuffy began to cement her place as leader, calling the others into line, even Lightning and Skitter. It became clear that they recognised Lilly and Squidge as part of their group, but they were most interested in Quetzee. To the point where they copied everything Quetzee did: washing themselves; mocking his high pitched call with their own, *prrztzz-prrztzz*; even going as far as mimicking the way he moved, holding four legs close to their bodies while walking with the other four.

And Quetzee called back.

Anything else that moved was stalked as food.

Mice, rats, guinea pigs, a fox, cats, dogs, and even Brian and Missy would be stalked from behind the Plastech of their enormous cage. Watching them, she worried about the wild dreadbeasts running somewhere in the facility – all alone.

Brian and Missy remained terrified – refusing to even enter the lab unless every single dreadbeast was locked up. (They also tried to insist Quetzee be caged, but Lilly drew the line at that.)

And maybe she couldn't entirely blame them for being cautious. Lilly found she was spending a lot of effort keeping the dreadbeasts and Quetzee apart. They were all so adorable, she couldn't bear the thought that the calls and chitters they made when Quetzee entered the room, were not in welcome. That the dreadbeasts might consider Quetzee prey.

Still, she couldn't hide from the fact that the dreadbeasts were designed to kill. What if they got out and killed Quetzee? Or Quetzee killed a dreadbeast? It was almost beyond thought. They were all just so adorable, she couldn't bear losing a single one. Chalky, Scratch, Skitter, Crunch, Tuffy, Runt, Lightning, Fang, she loved them all. Which was why she was devastated when the inevitable email arrived, reminding her once again of the side of her job that she would be most happy to forget.

§

To: MissLionheart@MrBig.net.www.e
From: MrBig@MrBig.net.www.e
CC: Lab2staff@MrBig.net.www.e
Subject: Dreadbeast Trial
Time: 24 Jan, 9:01

It is time to run preliminary trails for the ultimate showcase of the Criminal Mastermind world: The World Wide Web of Evil's Spring Exhibition. Your beasts must earn their plaice, or dye. Have them and the lions ready for the arena by the 28th of January.
I'm expecting big things. Let's see if we can find out why 28th of January is "fun at work" day.

Your Boss and Overlord,
Mr Big

§

Lilly groaned. Bad enough the pompous incompetent bully-boy was threatening her life, but did he have to be so cheesy about it?

With only four days left, she was still too terrified to put the dreadbeasts against a reasonable adversary – they looked so small against the larger predators. Even the mastiffs were almost three times their size—

What if Mr Big was right?

## •28•

# PRIDE

FOUR DAYS PASSED IN a mess of paperwork and half-completed projects. The dragon project mostly. Lilly spent every free moment frantically trying to ensure the dreadbeasts were ready for their big fight, which meant keeping Quetzee busy by sending him off to the menagerie to hunt.

After a heavy training session, and burnishing the dread-beasts' shells, she went to find Quetzee feeding on a war horse. Eyes rolling, she tried to rear, but her legs buckled and she fell against the bars of her cage. Quetzee remained on her back, happily feeding, as the horse struggled to right herself.

Lilly grabbed a dose of black widow antidote and injected the war horse as the horse's legs gave way, and wild eyed, she began to convulse.

Prrrting happily, Quetzee jumped off the writhing horse's back and onto Lilly's shoulders.

A deft little dose of sedative, to let the antivenin kick in, and the war horse would be right as rain. Lilly patted the poor creature until she stopped struggling, and her heartbeat slowed and steadied.

Then Lilly froze. From the top bars of the adjacent cage dangled some rather large and disconcerting strands of spider web. That cage should have held six wild pig-crocodile crosses – but she could only see four. *The missing dreadbeasts*? It had to be, she'd never seen spider web so thick, only the ones in captivity weren't showing any sign of using silk.

Lilly reached out and grabbed the sticky strand, shoving it quickly into her pocket as the door crashed open.

Veins and Basher, their faces still pocked with stitches, sauntered into the room with four large carry-cases. "Mr Big says we need your dreadbeasts now."

"Now? Just give me a moment."

"Right away, or there'll be trouble." Basher grinned as he hit his fist against his palm with a meaty thunk.

Reluctantly, Lilly took them over to the lab and opened the dreadbeasts' cage door. Not wanting any trouble, she even demonstrated how to move the rear cage wall forward so the dreadbeasts had no choice but to enter the strange new environment of the carry cases.

The dreadbeasts hissed and chattered angrily as Skitter and Chalky and Crunch were pushed into a carry case.

"Wait—" Lilly meant to say there was no need to crush three dreadbeasts into one carry case, when Quetzee yowled and clawed her shoulder. With no more warning, he jumped on Basher's arm and bit deep.

Basher grabbed Quetzee, and without even saying *ow*, prized Quetzee's jaws open, and stuffed him, yowling, into one of the cages. "Thanks," Basher sneered. "The boss said he needed this one too."

"No!" Lilly yelled. Desperate, she rushed up to Basher and grabbed his cold, dead, zombie arm. "Just the dreadbeasts. That was the deal. Give Quetzee back." She was so angry, it took a moment to realise something was odd. Not the cold under her fingers, she'd expected that. As she tried to wrest the cage from the zombie, she recognised what it was. Basher was still upright. When Quetzee bit someone, they normally reacted to the poison. Annoyingly, it was having no effect at all. *Stupid zombie.* She yanked the cage harder, upsetting Quetzee whose yowling reached fever pitch as he skidded around inside.

Lilly realised struggling with the cage wasn't helping, so she stepped back. Looking around wildly for help, she saw only Squidge, sitting at his computer. As usual, he was far too preoccupied to notice. Brian and Missy were probably still off on their mission fork-lifting the lions to the Monster Death Ring.

"You can't take Quetzee!" she yelled, wishing she had a knife on her. The only thing on hand was a state of the art sequencer – and throwing that was probably, no *definitely*, a bad plan. Then she realised there was at least one non-expensive piece of equipment nearby. A chair. She picked it up. "Give him back or … or I'll smash you over the head with this."

Veins stopped corralling dreadbeasts, took out a gun and trained it on her – then moved his sights to Quetzee with an evil smile. "I might not be authorised to shoot you, but I can certainly shoot your little pet."

"Yeah. We have our instructions. Either he goes in and fights the lions and the dreadbeasts, or he fights the little piece of lead in this gun here." Basher pulled his own gun and waved it about, before remembering he was a professional, and pointing it squarely at Quetzee. "It'll be like shooting rats in a barrel," he laughed.

"You can't! Not Quetzee! He can't win against lions *and* dreadbeasts, that's not fair!"

"Just watch us," Veins said. "Mr Big doesn't care what kills him, so long as he sees your horrid little fluff-ball turned into toast." He looked over at one of the pesky hovering camera eyes. "Besides, none of your creatures are much more than a bite-sized snack for the lions."

As if he knew what the zombie was saying, Quetzee lashed out at Vein's arm, screeching and spitting.

The dreadbeasts followed suit. Solidarity between the two very different types of animals? She hoped so. She'd coded for it, but still, behaviours were some of the trickiest things to get right. And she couldn't quite bring herself to trust that it had actually worked.

Two more camera eyes floated in to check out the racket Quetzee and the dreadbeasts were making.

She didn't care. "Necrotic nincompoops! Cretinous cadavers! Mictuating morts![36]" she yelled at them, angrily wiping tears from her eyes. Not that it did the least bit of good.

Basher slammed the cage door on the last of her dreadbeasts.

"Watch out! They're precious." Squidge yelled, finally surfacing from his dragon conundrum. Lame as it was, it was about the best backup she could hope from someone who hated confrontation.

"Please," Lilly begged as they started carting the cages out the door. "You have all the dreadbeasts. Don't make Quetzee fight too." She choked back a sob as the door swung back and almost hit her in the face. The sudden peak of adrenaline as she rocked out of the way shocked her. It was enough to transform her emotions from despair to a cold anger as she assessed the situation. Quetzee could not die. Would not die. He was tough. And so were her dreadbeasts. They would win. All of them. No point thinking about what she would do otherwise.

Squidge got up from his computer. "There, there," he said awkwardly. "The dreadbeasts will be alright. But we ... we

---

36 Necrotic is the scientific word for dead, usually used in reference to necrotic tissue or cells . Really the whole tirade shows an unreasoning dislike of zombies. *VF*

have to keep on working. Remember, as you said just the other day, the cure for crying is hard work."

"That was my parents. My foster parents," she corrected for the sake of the cameras. "Just another one of their lies."

"Maybe," Squidge said. "Maybe it was a lie. And maybe they were accidentally right anyway. Still, it is worth a try – and this dragon is not about to make itself."

Lilly forced a smile. "Thanks."

Squidge smiled back hesitantly, as if he was trying the expression on for size.

"Torpid tonsilloliths[37]," Lilly swore. Just being separated from Quetzee was breaking her heart. Mr Big would pay for this. The smug smarmy murderous bastard. He had her working for him, while the people who had raised her were in a cage to secure her good behaviour. She'd shied away from thinking about it for so long – not liking the horrible feeling of betrayal on all sides. Or that she couldn't find any way out of this mess. For her, her parents, her designer creatures, and for her team. But worst of all was not knowing if her whole life up to this point had been a sham.

She rubbed her face. Just like her critters, she had to be tough. Properly tough. Not just telling herself things didn't matter – but fixing them. She rushed out into the corridor, and yelled after Veins and Basher. "I want Quetzee back. I'll bring him to the fight myself."

"Sorry Miss, no can do," Veins said. "Wouldn't want anyone to say we'd cheated now, would we?"

"I don't need to cheat. My animals are the best."

"Then why're you making such a fuss?"

"Because you're pitting them against each other, and the lions, aren't you?"

"Haw, haw." Basher thumped her on the back. "You keep telling yourself that these pip-squeaks have a chance against

37 These foul smelling concretions formed from clusters of calcified material caught in tonsil crypts, are also called tonsil stones. *VF*

the lions."

They continued to trundle her critters, her babies, away.

Maybe she could have cheated? But how? She'd already conferred as many advantages on all her critters as she possibly could, anything more would be as dangerous to her charges as to their adversaries.

She went back inside the lab, found a mirror and cleaned herself up. A spy needed to look good. A genius needed to think smart and work hard.

That afternoon passed slowly in a haze of busy work and cleaning. Missy and Brian were uncharacteristically helpful, or maybe they'd been getting the hang of things for a while, and she hadn't noticed. In expectation of the oncoming fight, they demanded to pack up early.

"It won't be open yet," Lilly sighed.

Missy smiled. "What are you going to do here? Mope? Why don't we go to the Monster Death – I mean to the mess hall? We can at least make sure your Quetzee's being looked after *properly* before the fight."

Lilly couldn't help but be suspicious. "But I thought you didn't like Quetzee?"

Shrugging noncommittally, Melissa started to cadge Squidge. "You have to come too, Squidge. It's our unit on the line."

"Yeah," Brian said. He looked at Lilly with false wide-eyed innocence. "Maybe we could just … I don't know … make things a little easier for our critters."

Well, that explained it. They wanted to see if there was some advantage to be had. Cheat. Lilly shrugged, had to be worth a look. "Come on, Squidge, we might need you."

Squidge grudgingly packed away his computer. "Guess we should see how the fight is going to be set up."

Their whole team traipsed down the empty corridor,

only to find bookies loudly touting their odds to crowds of potential gamblers. Lilly elbowed her way through all the thugs, minions, and super-evil villainous types standing around laughing, gossiping and boozing. As she was fighting her way to the animal cages, Mr Big arrived in a flurry of haste and attendants.

The crowd parted to let him through.

He waddled up to the sound-stage and grabbed a microphone. "Friends, colleagues, minions, welcome to the fight of the century. My fight. I know you're thinking two lions against a pack of dreadbeasts is hardly fair no matter how small the dreadbeasts are. And that is why I purchased this little beauty."

"No," Lilly gasped as Mr Big unveiled a third lion. A young lioness.

Mr Big coughed, momentarily cutting through a flurry of betting in favour of the lions. "And just to make it interesting," he yelled into the mic, "and throw the bottlebrush in with the knives, so to speak, our very own Miss Lionheart's squirrel-thing is fighting as well. That'll stir things up a bit."

Mr Big cheerfully gave the mic to a fawning attendant and began betting on *his dreadbeasts*, laughing about how he didn't mind throwing good money after bad.

Lilly, standing nearby, couldn't believe it. Was all his negativity just for show? Or did he have another agenda? Why belittle her creatures, make it harder for them, and then bet on them? It didn't make any sense.

Almost nobody else followed suit, except of course, Lilly and her team. Squidge shrugged when someone asked him why he was betting for the dreadbeasts but against the squirrel thing. "I could always do with extra cash for the lab. Also, I am hoping the dreadbeasts will polish off that Quetzee at the same time. It is such a nuisance. Miss Lionheart spends her time looking after it, instead of working in the lab."

"All or nothing," Lilly said, cheerfully. To Missy's disbelief, she handed the bookie over the entirety of her earnings. "After all, if my critters die, I don't think I'm going to be hanging around."

The bookie accepted the money with a grin. "Don't see as how the dreadbeasts *and* the squirrel-beast can both win, lassie," he said.

She glared at him. "Who do you think you're calling *lassie*?" she muttered, but he'd already turned away to take the next eager gambler. Deva.

"Those runts?" Deva laughed when the bookie asked if she was going to bet on the dreadbeasts too. "They're so tiny. I'm betting on the big 'uns." She held out a hundred dollar note. I hear the lions have poison an' all – so those baby *dread* thingys are soon gunna be baby *dead* thingys soon enough."

The bookie laughed. "Hard to tell with the designers, lady. The big ones don't always do so well."

"Nah. The designers always lose," she said flatly. "Um ... ah." She looked around nervously. "I mean, I'm betting on them lions. Shoulda last time, too."

"What do you mean?" Lilly asked. But she got no answer, just, "sorry, gotta run, I'm s'posed to be on shift."

Missy pulled Lilly away. "Don't mind her," she yelled into Lilly's ear. "Let's find a good position near the action.

An impossible feat – all around the enclosure, people were pressed right up to the Plastech to watch. Lilly felt a little sick rise at the back of her throat. It was nerve wrecking, not knowing how the dreadbeasts would react to Quetzee in the heat of battle. Not knowing if the lions would get lucky and maybe kill one of her creatures. Yes, the lions might be works of mutant designer Paul the Poisoner and therefore creature art, and precious. And she'd hate to see them die – but they weren't *her* works of art. Besides, her babies needed to eat didn't they? That's the thing when you design savage meat-eating creatures. Other animals had to be sacrificed for the greater good.

Lilly bit her nails. A disgusting habit she thought she'd long since abandoned. But not today. Today she almost grabbed a cigarette out of someone's hand – and she'd never smoked before. Well, just the once, and it had made her sick for a week.

If only there was something she could do, other than wait and watch and cross her fingers that all the animals she loved, and of course her whole team, including the humans, would make it out of this alive.

Finally Mr Big raised his arms high, and an announcer's voice boomed out over the loudspeakers. "Ladiethugs and gentlethugs. It is my pleasure to announce that tonight we have something special in our Monster Death Ring.

"Paul the Poisoner's lions."

Well one of them obviously wasn't a Paul the Poisoner lion, but the crowd didn't seem to care about important details like that, not judging by its deafening cheer.

Mr Big dropped his right arm and an attendant raised the door between the lion's cage and the main arena.

That wasn't fair. But the three lions didn't move to take control of the new space. They hovered around their own gate, waving their ponderous heads to and fro, no doubt too upset by the noise to take full advantage of the terrain.

There was a hush of expectation.

"And Lilliana Lionheart's dreaded dreadbeasts!"

"All eight of the blighters!" Mr Big cut in. "*And* the ball-of-fluff squirrel-thing."

The crowd broke into laughter, and flooded the bookies with more bets.

*Yeah*, thought Lilly. *Nobody was laughing when he was on my shoulder, and they were walking by, were they?*

At last Mr Big dropped his other arm, and Quetzee and the dreadbeasts' cages were finally opened. Unlike the lions, the dreadbeasts swept into the centre of the Plastech arena, clattering across the floor, tongues flicking in excitement.

Seeing all the critters advancing toward them, the two lionesses snarled and padded cautiously out of their cage, the lion not so far behind.

"Prrrt," Quetzee called.

The lions and the dreadbeasts looked over at Quetzee, and hesitated. The dreadbeasts were the first to move, losing their strung out formation, and pouncing on Quetzee. Within moments he was overwhelmed.

"Quetzee!" Lilly screamed as he disappeared under a pile of dreadbeast carapaces.

The crowd roared.

Tears burned Lilly's cheeks. "Quetzee?!" she yelled, but he was gone. Trapped under so many, there was no chance he could get out without being bitten.

Sensing a change of atmosphere, the lions approached the dreadbeasts, warily flicking the critters with their enormous paws. Flicked into the air, a dreadbeast hissed, clattered across the floor, and bounced against a transparent wall.

Lilly didn't care, she turned away, boiling with a sudden hatred for the dreadbeasts. For everyone. But most of all for herself. How had she ever let Quetzee become involved in this? He was worth so much more.

•29•

# DEATH

"LILLY!" MISSY YELLED. "LOOK!"

"I don't want to watch," Lilly wailed. She didn't want to turn and see Quetzee mauled to death by all the dreadbeasts. Her dreadbeasts!

"But Miss Lilly!" Brian grabbed her. "Look!"

Missy was pointing into the fray.

Was that ... ?

"Prrrtssz." Quetzee's call could just be heard. It cut through the din, as he burst out from under the dreadbeasts.

"Prrrt prrrt." Quetzee called again, taking point against the three lions.

"Prrztzz-prrztzz," the dreadbeasts replied.

"He's alive! Go Quetzee!" Lilly yelled. "Go dreadbeasts!" Delightful creatures, how could she ever have doubted them?

A lioness snarled and lunged, missing Quetzee and batting an outlying dreadbeast. Scratch!

Lilly winced, trying to ignore the applause erupting from Dr Deathless' posse as Scratch tumbled across the floor – and smacked up against the wall.

Paul the Poisoner's lioness sniffed closer ... and snapped her jaws around the defenceless Scratch. Scratch's shrill shriek was cut short by an awful crunching noise, and vivid green ooze spilled from her broken body.

All around the audience went crazy. They were jumping up and down, patting each other on the back, and screaming for the lions to repeat the attack.

Lilly tried not to puke as the lioness coughed strings of light green mucous across the cage, then batted the inert Scratch with a paw.

Hearted by the success, the young lioness padded towards Quetzee.

"Bravo!" Mr Big yelled, and started clapping. Why was he so happy? He'd been betting on the dreadbeasts – hadn't he?

Then Lilly saw Chalky, Lightning and Fang, climbing the Plastech walls. "You clever things," she said, pleased her gecko genes were coming in handy after all.

Some minions were pointing, mouths open in shock. Others swarmed the bookies, asking to withdraw or change their bets. A speaker boomed, carrying Mr Big's voice over the roar of the crowd. "Ladiethugs and gentlethugs. You know the rules. Betting is closed, no exceptions. Now, shut up, and let me enjoy the fight."

Chalky dropped onto the lion's back – white-tipped legs digging deeply into the lion's fur as he sank his fangs into the feline's rump.

Unable to reach the biting nuisance, the lion roared, shaking his whole body. Snarling and twisting, he snapped frantically, his mane whipping from side to side with majestic vigour until Chalky flew off. He clattered against the wall of the cage, and crashed to the ground.

"Chalky!" Lilly yelled, as the lion pounced at his tormentor, his slavering jaws about to snap Chalky in two. Dodging claws and teeth, the feisty beast scampered clear, but Chalky wasn't her only favourite in danger—

Quetzee had made a mad dash under Paul's lioness still mauling Scratch.

Dropping the very dead dreadbeast, Paul's lioness bared her teeth … Lilly bit back a scream. One bite and Quetzee would be dead!

Sidestepping the lioness' jaws, Quetzee darted in and sank his fangs into her haunch.

The lioness howled, attention riveted on Quetzee, as, chittering happily, he scampered out of striking distance. Intent on Quetzee, she didn't notice the two dreadbeasts above her until they dropped on her back.

Howling, she bucked and leapt at Quetzee, the dreadbeasts bravely managing to hang on.

The lion padded over to join her, and together they both swiped at Quetzee – who darted away, unharmed.

"Prrrt Prrrt."

"Prrztzz-prrztzz," the dreadbeasts called back.

The lion swiped again – this time at the dreadbeasts on the lioness' back, and the dreadbeasts jumped clear.

Blood trickling down her flanks, the lioness rounded on the lion, snarling.

Bristling back, the lion flicked out his paw again, this time more as warning, than attack.

Quetzee dashed underneath him and sank his fangs into the exposed belly, scampering clear as the lion reared, his jaws snapping shut on air.

"Prrrt prrrt."

"Prrztzz-prrztzz," the dreadbeasts called back. And one – two – three dreadbeasts dropped onto the lion. Runt, Skitter and Lightning. Moments later they were flung clear across the floor. But that didn't seem to worry them. They unfolded their limbs, shook themselves indignantly, and re-entered the fray.

As the fight reached fever pitch, dreadbeasts were everywhere biting lions, and clattering across the floor and walls, even the ceiling as they were thrown clear.

Lilly cheered them all on ... then the young lioness picked up a stunned dreadbeast and crunched. "Skitter!"

Through her tears Lilly saw Skitter dragging himself along the floor – and up the wall. Tough, that one.

"Shouldn't the lions be showing signs of poisoning?" Brian asked.

Lilly, too concerned about the fight to think about framing a reply, bit her lip as Crunch darted towards the lioness.

"Any minute now," Squidge told Brian.

The young lioness flicked the unfortunately-named Crunch into her jaws and bit down hard.

"Holy guacamole," Melissa swore, as green-tinged saliva spurted over Crunch. Seconds later, coughing and sneezing, the lioness spat him out again.

He lay motionless in a puddle of gore,

*Crunch? Scratch? Dead?* Lilly thought in a daze, distantly aware of the crowd of minions all screaming with excitement.

Brian put an arm around her, and Missy followed suit. She'd rather they didn't, but at least they meant well.

Runt dashed up to the young lioness, sidestepping a brutal swat from her paw and darting off to climb the walls of the Plastech cage again. Using this distraction, Quetzee slunk underneath her belly, bit, and ran away.

Someone in the crowd booed, and Lilly thought she saw the lion stumble. Yes, he was dragging his hindquarters behind him, definitely showing signs of poisoning. Snarling and roaring and ineffectively shaking his mane as the creatures leapt onto him – and the lionesses trailing something behind them. Gossamer? Definitely silk. So the stuff in her pocket had been from one of the wild dreadbeasts. She put her hand in her pocket to feel how sticky and strong it was, but it was all tangled up, and impossible to tell if it would be strong enough to hold lions.

Quetzee battled on. Confined to the ground, he was exposed – and quick though he was, when two lionesses swiped at him, he couldn't dodge both. Paul the Poisoner's lioness sent him flying into a wall.

"Quetzee!"

Stunned, he scrambled upright, head wobbling.

The successful lioness swiped again. And Quetzee rolled away from the worst of the blow with a mournful, "prrrtssz."

"Prrztzz-prrztzz," the nimble Lightning jumped up onto the older lioness' shoulder, clinging to the attacking limb and sinking in her jaws.

The big cat roared and shook herself, but not quite so fiercely as she once had.

Lightning clung on, climbed a little higher, and bit again while Quetzee dashed in to nip at the lioness' flanks. Hindquarters collapsing, the Paul's lioness fought on, even as Tuffy tried to wrap her in sticky threads of silk.

Silk broke as the lioness struggled. *Would it really work?* The gossamer-fine strands didn't seem to be anywhere near strong enough to subdue a lion – until Runt and Chalky turned up and also began drawing silk from their spinnerets. With three dreadbeasts the silk held.

Paul's lioness roared a muffled roar, writhed a final time under layers of silk, and was still.

The lion was already wrapped so tight he looked like a giant plastic skittle with a lion's head poking out. Within moments, the young lioness had suffered the same fate.

Quetzee sat down by her silk encased shoulder with a delighted, "prrrt prrrt," and took the opportunity to avail himself of a good long drink from her carotid artery.

Mr Big clapped heartily, laughing at the grumbles of the once exuberant crowd. "Better luck next time, losers. Now, if you'll excuse me, I've got important business to attend to." He smiled at his bookie and the thug handed over Mr Big's winnings with a forced grin.

It was all over. People were filing out. And then Lilly realised her bookie was trying to escape with the crowd. If she didn't get her money now, she'd never see it again. Squidge also saw the danger. Between them they managed to cut him off from the exit. He scowled as he counted the large wad of money into her hands, before turning to Squidge with the same sullen glare. Squidge smiled politely back. "I do not see your problem. You did well today."

"Coulda done better," he muttered.

"Congrats," Missy said, swooping in on them. "Congrats to us all, nobody thought we could, but we did it!"

"Thanks, Missy." Lilly sighed. "Unfortunately, the hard work isn't over. We still need to rescue Quetzee and the dreadbeasts from this circus."

As they pushed their way back to rescue the animals, a security guard burst into the room. "Deva's gone missing. She's not at her post. We can't find her anywhere."

"Not Deva!" Missy whispered. "She was respected. Not the flaky type to run off."

"Quiet!" Mr Big yelled over the hubbub. "Security, I need a full detail, and a trace. Shoot her on sight! Move!" he yelled at the disappearing backs of three enormous thugs – people parting all around them as they set off for the exits.

"Why would he do that?" Melissa cried. "Deva wouldn't try to escape. She wouldn't … "

Brian stood with his mouth hanging open, even Dr Deathless looked as though he'd been stunned by a cattle prod.

Dear Diary,

Brian shifted all the dreadbeasts back to the lab with the forklift, and we held a moving funeral for Scratch and Crunch, then I went into the dreadbeast cage and polished the dreadbeast carapaces with a cloth, until they shone. By the end Quetzee was decidedly jealous. "Prrrtssz," he said, batting at the cloth in my hand.

I head-butted him and went to look for his brush. And told him how well he did. He chattered happily, and then I went back to the mess. Everyone was still on edge because of Deva's disappearance, and rumours abounded – Deva had escaped – she was making a leadership bid – someone had shot her in the back and fed her to the dinosaurs.

I told everyone I'd seen her betting earlier, and what would be the point if she was planning something? She must have been attacked.

Squidge thought she might have been trying to create an alibi.

Melissa disagreed with everyone. Insisting something was catastrophically wrong. Deva would never try to escape and she would never desert her post. But even though I scoffed, I still worried about what that something catastrophic might be. I mean people die in this place all the time. But usually they don't just disappear. Had somebody – or something, had killed Deva? But how? And how did Melissa know Deva well enough to be sure she wouldn't escape?

Still, through all the drama – and even through the tears of losing two beautiful dreadbeasts – I couldn't stop smiling. We'd survived! I was so proud of my team.

But most especially I was proud of my designer creatures. They were eating and grooming together like one big happy family.

It had taken me too long to conquer my fear they might eat each other, because I couldn't bear the thought of losing Quetzee – so maybe it was for the best that Mr Big had insisted he enter the ring. No, it was definitely for the best. Without Quetzee it would have been a far more even fight. More of my precious dreadbeasts might have died.

But then I'd rather they didn't have to fight at all. No, now isn't the time to think about such things, I have a success to celebrate with my team. And all my surviving critters to look after.

It was a sad day, and I'll never forget Scratch and Crunch, but there will be time to mourn for them again later. Now it is time for some well-earned celebration.

§

To: Your Boss and Overlord
From: Security
Subject: Notify me immediately—
Date: 28 Jan, 11:57

We've found Deva's body in a linen closet west corridor wrapped in some kind of sheet. Bring back-up, we're going in.

# •30•

# FALL

AT BREAKFAST THE NEXT morning the only thing anybody talked about was that people were disappearing, and not just Deva. Everyone was so jumpy that when Lilly dropped her spoon, half the room leapt out of their seats. The cafeteria was definitely emptier than usual, and rumours abounded – escalating from an escape, to a full-blown plot, to the bunker being under attack from another WWWOE faction.

It was hard not to panic. Why did this have to happen now, just when her designer animal project was going so well? Unless it was the escaped dreadbeasts. But she wasn't ready, she hadn't planned for this. Not yet. She'd spent last night celebrating, and now, in all the stress, it was hard to think straight.

A dragon-tattooed minion at the next table comforted a terrified co-worker. "Don't worry, they'll find the culprits, Mr Big's ordered a massive search. Every room will be searched until the agents are found."

Damn. Mr Big would find the lost dreadbeasts – and the deaths would be blamed on her and her team.

The minion kept on talking. "If it was an outside attack, we'd all know by now."

"You mean we'd be dead."

"Yeah, I guess. At least it would be quick. With this, who knows? The boss gets nervous, and things could get very messy."

Suddenly Lilly wasn't hungry any more.

She walked back to work, and took a moment to fuss over the dreadbeasts, encouraging them to practise their jumping. Quetzee helped by leaping around the lab desks until Brian arrived and she had to lock them all in their cage.

Half an hour later, Missy still hadn't arrived.

"You think she's okay?" Brian asked. "She has to be okay. She couldn't have died, could she?"

"She might have escaped," Lilly said with an outrageous hopefulness. Unlikely as it was, she wanted it to be true. And why not? Maybe Missy wasn't a genius, but, however hard she tried to hide it, she was quite clever.

Squidge shrugged. "Maybe she barricaded herself in her room to wait for all the fuss to blow over. I would have, if I was not so busy with the dragon project."

"That's nice," Lilly said. She thought she could hear screaming in the distance, but as this was an evil villain's underground bunker, she decided Squidge and Brian were right, and the better part of valour was not to investigate.

It hardly mattered, Dr Deathless came in a few moments later, white as a sheet, spider-web dripping from one hand – a flame gun in the other.

"You!" He waved the flame gun at Lilly. "I told your parents this was a bad idea. I can't protect you any more. But I guess they knew that when they skedaddled."

"They left me here? You mean they escaped, and no one told me?" Lilly asked, flabbergasted, before deciding that wasn't what she was really surprised about. "*You!?* You were protecting *me*?" She'd never thought for a moment he might be the person passing all those notes to her in the early days – not even after he'd bumped into her.

She should have guessed it when he *let slip* the information on echo-location – he'd pretty much handed that to her on a plate. Probably wanted the maps himself – or he'd arranged for her to see her parents – or, maybe, he simply hadn't realised they were a trap. In some ways it was a tragedy all his planning had been for nothing.

Deathless shook his head. "You've got no information for me, have you? Girl, you might be a genius, but you're also a fool. Don't know what anyone ever saw in you. You're not cut out to be a spy, so much as WWWOE fodder. What a mess, I'll have to tell your fosters you're a lost cause," he muttered. "Be lucky to survive this myself without you dragging me down." He chucked an explosive out the door, waited for the – *boom!* – and ducked out into the corridor.

"What was that about?" Brian asked.

Lilly shrugged. "Apparently my parents got me into all this. Thought I'd be a great spy or something. I seem to have disappointed them."

"It was a clever plan." Squidge, for once, was listening so intently, he was even looking at her.

"Yeah, except for me being a spy. And working for a megalomaniac. All their planning, and what's it got them?"

"Yes. Hard to say. They could have escaped," Squidge admitted. "But they are equally likely to have made it into the shark tank, or down a death pit."

"Thanks for that," Lilly muttered.

Squidge smiled. "Any time."

As if sensing her distress, Quetzee nosed in and jumped on her lap, snuggling in with a *prrrt prrrt*.

"Good boy," she said picking up her diary, pen poised over the pages – wondering what she could possibly write to allay suspicion for just a moment longer – when Mr Big barged in, Annie straining at the leash.

It was almost a relief, until she saw everyone trailing in after him – Basher, Veins, Pinhead, and two enormous thugs, followed by a crying Missy. Three camera eyes tumbled ominously in their wake, like a small swarm of overexcited silver jellyfish.

Lilly jumped off her seat and cowered backward, holding Quetzee firmly in her arms. His ears were pricked, and his tongue flicked in and out. In that moment it finally registered there was no escape.

"Idiot!" Mr Big yelled, pointing at the cage behind Lilly. "One of those dreadbeasts was found with the desiccated corpse of my second favourite dog."

"And four people," Pat growled. "It took three of us to kill it."

"That's terrible," Lilly said, trying not to think about the poor dreadbeast's last moments.

Squidge ducked behind his computer. Brian hunkered behind the steriliser. But Lilly remained where she was. She'd taken her chances, rolled the dice, and now there was nothing else to do but see just how overwhelming a force Mr Big had brought against her. His oversized guards, his even more oversize Rottweiler, and most hated of all, Pat Pinhead and his worse-for-wear zombies.

Lilly had always known it was a matter of time before Mr Big decided she was expendable, but now the moment was here, she wasn't ready. Obviously. Because if she'd organised this properly she'd be busy sunning herself on a beach far, far away from here. Shaking, she held Quetzee tight, and cowered back to the cages along the wall.

All her plans, thoughts and contingencies evaporated, collapsing into one crazy opportunity. Her mind whirled.

"Missy, you were their spy? You've been reporting to them the whole time?"

Missy nodded. "I—"

"It's okay," Lilly said.

"Damn right it's okay." Mr Big barked. "I own the surly cow. I own the lot of you."

Missy flashed Mr Big a look of horror before turning to Lilly. "Sorry."

As Mr Big approached, the scuttle of many legs across the cage floor behind Lilly reminded her of everything she had to lose.

Time to make her stand. "I made the creatures you asked, Mr Big. I did what you … "

He sneered, fumbling with Annie's collar.

So this was how it was going to go. Lilly cringed, knowing everything has to fall at some point. And everyone.

"I love you." Sadly, Lilly kissed Quetzee on the nose and let him go.

Quetzee skittered away in a flash, dodging badly-aimed bullets and chittering shrilly. He ducked under Annie as the dog's collar clicked open—

As Annie leapt, Lilly reached behind her and tugged on the catch to open the dreadbeast cage.

The door caught.

Lilly tugged desperately, as rotten dog's breath washed over her and Annie landed on her chest. Heavy paws pushed the air from Lilly's lungs, and slavering jaws snapping inches from her face.

Blindingly fast, two dreadbeasts scampered over Lilly, and sank their fangs into Annie. Poor Annie yelped, and turned her attack from Lilly to the dreadbeasts. By the time the pack had bounded over the dog, her legs had buckled, and she'd collapsed to the ground.

The thugs stopped shooting at Quetzee through tables, and focused on the six oncoming dreadbeasts. Holding their ground like professionals.

Mr Big stepped behind them and pushed one of the oversized thugs into the path of the swarming dreadbeasts. And then, just to be sure, he pushed the other one as well.

The first thug fell, screaming unintelligibly, as, forked tongues flickering, the dreadbeasts took him down, barely pausing before moving on.

The second thug's legs soon buckled, and he too collapsed, frothing at the mouth.

Immune to poison, the zombies helped Pinhead put up a creditable fight (while Mr Big backed closer and closer to the door). Try as they might, the dreadbeasts were too fast. The zombies might be unfazed by poison, but even they were hampered as sheets of spider web began to fall.

Now bullets were no longer flying all around, Quetzee, jumped onto Pinhead's shoulder, and chomped down hard. Pinhead's final scream little more than a death rattle as he dropped to the ground.

Seeing the big man fall, Mr Big stopped backing off slowly, and began to run. He made it as far as the door before Lightning and Skitter overtook him and began festooning him in silk.

"I should have killed you earlier," Mr Big snapped. "All you ingrates," he said, staring at Missy wrapped safely in Brian's arms.

Draped in sheets of spider web, Mr Big struggled futilely to reach his feet, or maybe to reach a weapon – refusing to give in, even after Quetzee nipped him.

Lilly swallowed, looking around at the devastation, and at the gaggle of cameras. WWWOS Rule No 1. Don't be noticed – but if you are – create a lasting impression. "Fool,"

Lilly said. "If you wanted to kill me, you should have done it earlier. You know, before I'd created my army of dreadbeasts."

There was no reply, just a soft choking sound as Mr Big was engulfed in silk.

Squidge finally looked up from his hiding place. "Oh no, Miss Lionheart. The dreadbeasts have killed Mr Big. And Missy's back again."

"I'm sorry," Missy repeated.

"For what?" Squidge asked. "You were only doing your job, wasn't she, miss?"

"Hmm," Lilly said, surveying the room. Corpses were scattered from the dreadbeast cages to the door, with blood splattered over the floor and many of the tables. It was a scene from a nightmare.

Still, there was no time for tears, no time to soak up the enormity of what she'd done, and no escaping this. She had killed the boss. No super-villain in their right mind would ever let her go free now.

Lilly had no choices left. She had made her stand, and now there was only one way for her, let alone her team, to get out of this alive.

Squidge frowned. "And the dreadbeasts killed Pinhead and all his thugs. But they were not very nice, were they? Not like Missy. Missy is nice."

"Very observant, Squidge," Lilly said. If she was going to live, she needed to make the stakes clear. "Just don't think of this as killing the boss, think of it as … restructuring."

"What? Like business?" Squidge asked.

"Precisely," Lilly said. "What do you think, Missy?"

Missy looked nervously at Tuffy and Runt, chowing down on the rapidly desiccating corpse of Mr Big. She kicked Mr Big. "I don't really *like* business."

Lilly smiled. "Totally understandable. But it's a bit like

mucking out cages – something that has to be done if we want our animals looked after properly." Yes, that was definitely true. The menagerie could be so much better. A more stimulating, happy place.

"Besides, don't you think I'll make a far better super-villain than Mr Big? He only had an ego big enough to collapse a white star and a penchant for slightly dangerous critters – and maybe a few sharks. On the other hand, I can be a seriously awesome super-villain, because I can make properly dangerous animals that understand a chain of command."

"Okay, this may be a dumb question, but why am I still alive?" Missy asked.

"Good point." Lilly smiled. "But I'm just returning a favour, because I seem to remember when the dreadbeasts were dicey, and Mr Big was threatening to kill us, you kept us alive. Last time though, you hear?"

Missy nodded.

"Are you sure you really want to be a super-villain?" Brian asked. "Not that your animals aren't super-dangerous," he added quickly.

Lilly thought for a moment. Her childhood self was probably not completely wrong – there were some very important attributes that, as a super-villain, she needed to have. So maybe it was best to just to admit the obvious. "Well, apart from my superlatively dangerous animals, I do have an ego big enough to collapse a white star … And, I guess, a screwed up childhood." She frowned, and nodded to Missy. "Took me a while to realise just how screwed up. So thanks for that."

Squidge nodded his head wisely. "Miss Lionheart, I think you are right."

"Of course I'm right. But if I am going to take over, I've got a lot to do. I'm not sure everyone is going to take the news of a change of leadership quite as well as you are."

"I am," said Brian, waving his hand in the air and attracting the attention of the dreadbeasts.

"Good," Lilly said. "Just watch out, I think Tuffy wants to say hello."

Quetzee ran up, nuzzled Tuffy, then looked expectantly at Brian and Missy.

Brian and Missy held very still as, with a friendly prrztzz-prrztzz, Quetzee jumped onto Brian's shoulder and licked him. Tuffy followed suit and jumped up on Missy.

"I think they've decided to like you after all," Lilly said. "But that's enough chit chat. If we're going to make this take over a success, we can't muck around. So if you wouldn't mind, can you guys clean up this mess?" She waved at the bodies littering the floor. "And by the way, I'd appreciate it if you could set up a few more dreadbeasts. I'm sure we can order in some more snake eggs shortly."

"Yes, sir," Missy and Brian said in unison.

Squidge frowned in thought. "Miss Lionheart, dreadbeasts are only small-fry. You may not think a dragon is possible, but I would like to try."

"Good idea, Squidge. Maybe a little redesign first though," Lilly said. "I can think of a few tweaks that will make the project go much more smoothly."

Watching Runt and Fang finishing off their dinner, she'd realised that feeding all the dreadbeasts might become quite difficult, especially if they grew to the size she expected. And, of course, feeding a dragon would be harder still – assuming Squidge could make one. But, all in all, Lilly couldn't help but think there were plenty of people who would do the job very nicely …

She looked right into the eye of one of the cameras and yelled, “You just wait!” at the contraption as it whirred right up to her face. Then she grinned for the benefit of the techies, and any security, who might be watching. “If you thought this place was bad-ass when Mr Big was running it, well, I’ve got news for you. Now there’s a real mad scientist in charge – we’re going to be unstoppable.”

§

THE END …

… of the beginning. Watch out for more mayhem in the world of Miss Lilly Lionheart

Also by A.J. Ponder

*Wizard's Guide to Wellington*

You Choose Which Way Interactive Story
*Once Upon a Time*

§

Coming Soon

*Quest*

*Wizard's Guide to London*

You Choose Which Way Interactive Story
*Return to Once Upon a Time*

You Choose Which Way Interactive Story
*Web of Evil*

You Choose Which Way Interactive Story
*Web of Spies*

*Miss Lionheart's Laboratory*

Printed in Great Britain
by Amazon